To a fellow
mystery writer

In the Game
A Mystery

by

Peter G. Pollak

DEDICATION

To my unwitting mentors: Thomas Wolfe, Isaac Asimov,
Joseph Conrad, W. Somerset Maugham, Upton Sinclair, Jack
London, John Cheever, Thomas Mann, Ursula LeGuin,
Samuel R. Delany, Bill Kennedy and dozens like them.

ACKNOWLEDGMENTS

This book would not have seen the light of day without the help of a number of people, including faithful readers—Barbara Sullivan, Connie Jo DiCruttalo, Pat Capano, and Jude Ferraro. Their feedback convinced me that the novel was ready to be published.

Dr. Curtis Mills helped me with medical information and Susan Uttendorfsky of *Adirondack Editing* prevented me from making more errors than I want to admit.

No work of the mind is ever perfect. All remaining grammatical errors, typos or other errors are fully my responsibility.

Once again I have the good fortune to be able to thank Kelly Mullen of *InVision Studios* for the cover design and Michael Bagnardi, who contributed the cover illustration.

PROLOGUE

February 20, 1992: 11:15 a.m.

"Can't you move any faster?"

Bernard turned to look back, slowing himself down even more. Joanne had to brace herself to avoid running into him. "It's not good to get overheated, Jo," he replied.

She gave him a dirty look. She hated being called 'Jo'. "Fine," she said. "Let's keep moving."

Bernard winced. He knew that Joanne was a superior athlete when he suggested cross-country skiing in Thatcher Park, east of Albany, but he hoped his taking the initiative would change her attitude toward him. He should have realized that it was hopeless. After their third date, she had started measuring him, telling him in not-so-subtle ways where he came up short. She was hypercritical; it was probably why she chose law as a profession. Which begged the question: Why was he attracted to women like Joanne in the first place?

After a while, Bernard slowed down again. "Ready for lunch? There are some picnic tables up ahead."

Joanne nodded and gave him one of her thin smiles. That had been the first clue. He remembered when he first noticed her pretending. They seemed to hit it off on their first date. A few weeks after that, he took her to his favorite restaurant. He prided himself on his cooking skill and was planning to cook a meal for her, which he hoped would lead to intimacy, but when he started describing his version of one of the recipes on the menu, she seemed miles away. Her smile feigned attention while her eyes were roaming the room. Was she looking to see if she recognized anyone? Maybe she was rehearsing what she'd say about having been seen out with a divorced dentist. Instead of throwing in the towel, however, he tried harder to win her favor. He stopped talking about his cooking prowess and asked her what she liked to cook.

"What? Oh, I don't do very much cooking these days," she replied. "I pretty much stick to salads with chicken, or frozen fish. That is, if I even bother."

Bernard raised an eyebrow. "I'm sure you're being modest."

"No, it's true. Thank goodness for the Super Shopper. It's so easy to pick up something after work."

"I like to plan my meals a week at a time," he admitted.

Joanne had winked. "My, won't you make some woman a good catch!"

He remembered having smiled at her jibe, but he had been seething. Today's outing was probably his last chance.

Bernard took off his skis and started sweeping the loose snow off the picnic table. Joanne cleaned the bench on the opposite side.

"There's room enough for both of us on this side," he pointed out.

"I'm fine over here," Joanne replied, continuing to clear a space. She had been avoiding close physical contact from the moment he showed an interest. Yet, she kept saying yes when he asked her out, and, against his better judgment, he kept asking.

He had packed lunch the night before. Knowing she was not a sandwich eater, he purchased containers of humus and guacamole and cut up celery, carrots, and both green and red peppers. He also cut up chunks of Gorgonzola and had picked up some pita bread to go with it.

"I decanted a nice California merlot," he said, putting two wine bags on the table.

"Everything looks yummy," Joanne admitted.

He showed her how to open the wine bag, and then lifted his to his mouth. "*Salud*!"

"*Salud*," she replied.

They ate in silence for a few minutes.

"Bernard, this is so lovely. It's a perfect day. I want to thank you for suggesting it."

"I knew you'd like it," he stated.

"You're a sweet guy, Bernard, but I've been meaning to tell you. You're just not my type. I think this should be our last date."

Bernard nodded and looked down at his food. What was someone supposed to say at a moment like this?

"Don't feel bad," Joanne said. "I know you're coming off a divorce and you're probably looking for a long-term relationship. I'm sure you'll find the right woman soon. That's why it's better for you to keep looking than to waste your time with me."

He managed a sort of a smile. "Thanks for . . ." He was about to say 'nothing,' but realized that didn't sound right. "Thanks for being so honest," he mumbled.

Joanne smiled back. She lifted her wine pouch. "To finding a mate for Bernard." He lifted his pouch and drank, but felt foolish. He wanted to end the day then and there, but that would just confirm her view of him. He'd play the devil-may-care role to the end.

"Ready?" Bernard said a few minutes later, packing up the remainder of their lunch. "There's a spectacular view of the valley up ahead."

He swung the pack on his back and pulled on his ski gloves. "I'll follow you."

They skied steadily for the next hour, following the trail along the side of the ridge. The day had been cool and overcast to start, but was now sunny and getting warmer. Bernard's emotions were running riot. He hated himself for having thought she would fall for him. Things had come too easy. They'd been introduced at the singles club and she accepted his phone call inviting her out cheerfully. He also hated her for continuing to date him if she didn't feel they were compatible. But that was silly, he realized. The whole idea of the club was to meet people and to get to know them. You had to go out with someone a few times in order to get to know someone, didn't you? But she really didn't know him! She had judged him without giving him a chance. That wasn't fair.

A cliff ran along the side of the trail to their left, but a line of trees blocked the view. Joanne slowed down, then stopped where some people had created a side trail to the edge of the cliff. "Let's take a look," she said.

"What a view," Joanne said when she got to the edge.

Bernard was afraid of heights. He couldn't go over to the railing on the glassed-in deck at the Empire State Building. He remained several ski lengths back from where Joanne was leaning on her skis.

She turned back and waved her arm. "Come on, scaredy cat. It's a spectacular view."

Bernard shook his head. He saw a look of disdain as she turned away from him. A feeling of anger welled up in him. He braced his poles and pushed himself forward. The tops of her skis were inches from the edge of the cliff. Bernard let go of his ski pole, put his hand on her back, and pushed hard.

"What?" Joanne gulped as she turned to try to see what was happening. She tried to stop herself from falling, but it was too late. She screamed as she tottered on the edge, a look of incomprehension in her eyes. The scream became a shriek as her body plunged down the embankment.

Peter G. Pollak

1

Tuesday, April 13, 1999: 8:15 a.m.

"Dad, do you have any plans for today?"

Jake Barnes looked up from his newspaper. "Not yet."

"I made a list of some groceries we need. Where should I put it?"

"Right there on the counter."

"Don't forget to use the coupons from the Sunday paper."

Jake nodded. His daughter finished packing her lunch. She ate in her office at the back of the dress shop she managed in uptown Albany. "You'll be home when Michael gets out of school, right?"

Jake, who had gone back to his paper, looked up again. Mary was standing by the back door with her bags in hand. "Yes, Mary," he said, smiling.

"See that he takes Benji for a walk and finishes all of his homework before he watches any TV."

"Mary, dear, I know the routine."

"Then why did I find the two of you watching *The Simpson's* yesterday when he hadn't finished his math problems?"

"That was my fault. I told him to come down to help me get dinner ready."

Mary gave him a quizzical look. "So, what are you going to do today?"

"I thought I'd start by reading the newspaper and drinking a cup of coffee."

"You know what I mean."

"How about if I take up quilting? I hear they're starting a class at the community college."

"Dad, I'm serious."

"Mary. Please don't worry about me. I'll be fine."

Mary came over and gave her father a hug as best as she could while balancing her pocketbook, lunch bag, and briefcase.

Jake got up and opened the back door for her. He watched until she'd backed her car out the driveway, then after filling up his coffee mug, he snuck a doughnut from the box he'd hidden in the pantry, despite knowing he shouldn't be eating doughnuts period, and that third cup of coffee was probably bad for him as well. His doctor told him he needed to lose twenty-five pounds, but he didn't have the willpower these days. Staying in shape had seemed selfish four years ago when his wife became ill, and now, six months after her death, he still couldn't motivate himself to go to the gym.

Having finished reading the sports and news pages, Jake turned to the Life section. He had started reading that part of the newspaper after his wife had taken ill and he took over cooking duties. The paper offered quick and easy recipes that even he could manage. Then, after Mary's divorce, she moved back home with his ten-year-old grandson and Jake had volunteered to be in charge of evening meals during the week.

The obits were in the back of the Life section. Skimming to see if he recognized any names, a headline caught his eye. "Local Woman Dies in Mexico; Group Cuts Trip." He read the full story through quickly, then more slowly a second time.

Oaxaca, Mexico: Angela Boyer, 34, died Sunday after a brief illness while on a trip with the Albany Singles Club, a club official reported yesterday. Preliminary indications are that Boyer contracted spinal meningitis in a remote area in the Mexican state of Oaxaca.

"Angela Boyer succumbed despite receiving medical attention to combat the infection," reported Albert Blaylock, an official with the club, in a written statement. Blaylock, a local travel agent, was not on the trip.

The remaining members of the group will return home after undergoing medical tests in Mexico, according to the statement.

In addition to Boyer, the following Albany-area residents were on the trip: Ellen Bartlett, Karen Crosetti, Marlene Fitzpatrick, Beverly Harris, Dr. Bernard Johns, Elliott Jorgensen, Jessica Kennedy, Ed Martin, Marc Nicholson, William Parsons, Charlotte Richards, Susan Stachowski, Dr. Randolph Smythe, Ralph Thompson, and Stacey Winthrop.

"Damn! Damn! Damn!"

Benji, the Barnes' seven-year-old collie who had been asleep under the table, stirred, stretched, and got to his feet. Jake rubbed the dog's head. A sour feeling spread throughout his body like a fast-acting medication; he began to perspire. "I can't effing believe it."

Jake didn't know Angela Boyer. Nor, for that matter, did he know any of the other names listed at the bottom of the obituary—except for one—Dr. Bernard Johns, a local dentist he had questioned seven years previously when a woman with whom Johns had been skiing fell to her death in Thatcher Park. Jake had never been satisfied with Dr. Johns' rendition of what happened. He claimed he was watching from ten feet away when the woman lost her balance and fell. Even though his superiors at the Albany Police Department had declared the woman's death an accident, clearing Johns of any wrongdoing, Jake felt they had closed the investigation too early.

That case would have remained filed among the many others where the pieces don't quite fit, except for a second instance of an unexplained death with a connection to Dr. Johns. The body of a local woman was found at the bottom of a mountain trail in the Catskill region of New York State three and a half years ago. There were no obvious signs of foul play and again, the death was ruled an accident. Jake thought it suspicious that a hiking club member would have gone up a difficult trail without a companion. Following his hunch, Jake had obtained a list of the hiking club's members. One name stuck out: Dr. Bernard Johns.

Dr. Johns was divorced, had no children, and was a respected member of the Albany community. When Jake questioned the leader of the hiking club, he admitted having seen Johns and the deceased leave group meetings together. Jake filed his report with Lieutenant Art Keller, head of the Detectives' Bureau of the Albany Police Department, recommending that Johns be questioned in the woman's death, but Keller nixed the idea. The State Police had declared the woman's death accidental, Keller reminded Jake. Therefore, their department did not have an open case on the matter and he was not to interview Dr. Johns.

Now Johns' name had come up again in connection with the death of yet another area woman.

Taken separately, each of the three deaths might seem to have logical explanations, but Jake hadn't been a cop for thirty years without learning to detect guilt in a person's bearing. Something in Johns' demeanor had bothered him on that cold February afternoon seven years ago when he and his partner questioned Dr. Johns.

He still remembered Johns' exact words: "If she hadn't been so anxious to get a better view, she'd be alive today. Some women don't know when to stop." Later when he asked him to describe Feldman, he included the word "pushy" along with smart, athletic and attractive.

Had the fact that he'd gotten away with murdering Joanne Feldman emboldened Johns to commit additional murders? Was Angela Boyer yet another of his victims?

The question was, what could he do about it and why should he bother? Jake had been forced to retire from the Albany Police Department three months earlier after having failed a medical exam. He had been given the choice of going out on disability or retiring. He chose the latter. As a result, he had no legal standing to investigate Bernard Johns on his own, and he doubted that Art Keller would welcome his suggestion that someone look into what happened to Angela Boyer.

Maybe he should just forget about Bernard Johns, but he knew he couldn't do that. If Johns was guilty of even one murder, Jake wasn't going to be able to sleep at night if he didn't do something to bring him to justice. It didn't matter if he was off-duty. He still had an obligation to the victims, their families, and the community. It was his community, too.

The question Jake had asked himself over and over was "why?" Why would a prominent dentist kill any one of those women? Without a motive, Jake knew his chances of getting anyone else to take his questions seriously were slim to none. The answer to that question, if there was one, required police work. That's what Jake knew it would take, and bad heart or not, he was going to do what he did best.

Noticing that Benji was scratching at the back door to go out, he reluctantly reached for his jacket. "Okay, Benji. Time for your walk."

They were back in the family kitchen forty-five minutes later. Jake read the newspaper story one more time, stuffed his daughter's grocery list in his pocket, found his car keys, and headed out the back door.

Jake backed his Ford pickup truck out of his driveway. The grocery list that his daughter had left for him was clipped to the visor, but instead of driving in the direction of the nearest supermarket, he headed downtown to the headquarters of the Albany Police Department.

Art Keller would not be happy to see him. He might even guess the purpose of his visit before he had a chance to state his case. Just to be able to pull Keller's chain, he wished he could think of a reason for popping in to headquarters other than wanting Keller to investigate Johns' possible role in Angela Boyer's death.

When he got to the station house, Jake waved to the sergeant on duty at the front desk and headed back to the Detectives' Bureau.

Eddie Jamison, a relative newcomer on the squad, was sitting in the bullpen staring at a monitor. Jamison would have you believe that modern cops could solve crimes by sitting at computers. "What's up?" Jamison inquired.

Jake thought for a moment about suggesting that he should look into Angela Boyer's death, but Art Keller would have to approve the investigation and would realize that Jake had put him up to it. Better do his own dirty work.

"I'm here to see the lieutenant. Is he in?"

Jamison shrugged his shoulders. "His door's open. Must be around here someplace."

Jake wandered back to Keller's office, took a deep breath, and knocked on the door. No answer. He knocked again louder. Still no answer. He pushed on the door, opening it wide enough to stick his head around the door. There was no one at the desk.

"That's breaking and entering, Barnes," said a voice behind him.

Jake turned quickly, bumping his head against the doorjamb.

"Watch yourself," Lieutenant Keller said. "You're no longer eligible for disability."

Jake put his hand on his head. There was no blood, but it would be black and blue. "Hello, Art."

"You here to see me?" Keller asked, pushing the door open and going inside.

"I am."

Keller took off his jacket and hung it on the back of his wooden desk chair. "I'm afraid to ask."

"Did you see today's paper?"

"I did. Knicks lost again. They need a new center."

"You read the obits?" Jake asked, not wanting to get into a discussion about sports teams.

"You here to confess? Let me guess. You knocked off the old lady who charged you for a doughnut down at Wiggie's?"

He gave the lieutenant a thin smile, then went over and sat, uninvited, in the chair facing Keller's desk. He took a deep breath. "Did you take note of who was on that trip to Mexico with the woman who died?"

"Yes, Dr. Randolph Smythe. Let's hope his malpractice insurance is paid up or we might have to put him on suicide watch."

"I'm referring to the other medical professional."

"Let me guess. Your favorite dentist, no doubt?"

"You don't find that significant?"

"What would make it significant in my mind, Barnes, is if no one in the entire city of Albany ever died unless they were in the presence of the dangerous Dr. Johns. Otherwise, you'll just have to face the facts that not everyone dies in bed of old age."

"And when three otherwise perfectly healthy women, all of whom have a connection to Dr. Johns, die unusual deaths, you don't find that a bit odd?"

"What I find odd is that a certain disabled detective has not moved to Florida and learned to play golf, and I find it odd that he wants to continue to play policeman when the taxpayers of Albany are perfectly happy to pay him to stay home."

"Did they do an autopsy?"

"I don't know and before you ask me to order one, the answer is no."

Jake pulled at his collar. "Have you inquired whether there is a police report available to see whether Dr. Johns was even questioned?"

"What I do not understand, Barnes," Keller said, making no effort to keep his voice down, "is why you have developed an obsession about a man who is a respected member of the community, who has never been issued so much as a traffic violation, and who will sue this department six ways to Sunday if I ever take your suggestion seriously."

The veins on Keller's neck were taut and his face was a deep red. He took a deep breath. "And, if you don't hi-tail it out of my Bureau, I'm going to buzz downstairs to Sergeant Bittner and inform him that he's going back on night duty for having let you come back here in the first place."

"I can see that you're not open to reason, Art. I'll leave, but I hope you're not going to be sorry you didn't look into this guy."

Jake repressed the urge to slam Keller's door on the way out. He noticed Jamison looking his way with a smirk on his face.

"Enjoy that Jamison?" he asked. Without waiting for an answer, he walked out of the Bureau, leaving the door open so that Jamison would have to get up to close it.

"Jake. Jake Barnes!" someone called to him as he reached the street.

Jake turned around. It was Curt Ellis, a member of the department with whom he'd worked on several cases over in the troublesome South End. "Curt. How are you doing?"

Jake shook Ellis' hand. Ellis was dressed in a light blue suit set off by a dark blue shirt with a white collar and a red tie. "You're looking pretty spiffy," Jake said when he caught his breath. "Got a court appearance?"

"Nah. I'm no longer on the job."

"I didn't know. Me neither. Retired."

"Yeah, I heard. I resigned two months ago. I got tired of being passed over for promotions, if you know what I mean."

Jake nodded. Ellis had always impressed him as being a good cop—someone who ought to move up in the ranks. He wondered if Ellis thought his being black worked against him. "So what are you doing these days?"

"I'm a PI for a big law firm—Marks, Kelleher, Hacker & Wilson. You've heard of them?"

Jake nodded. They were one of the biggest and connected politically to the Democratic Party, which had run Albany for the past sixty years. "How's that going for you?"

Ellis smiled. "Better hours and not as dangerous. I do things like follow guys who are cheating on their wives, but I don't have to arrest them or try to break up the fight when the wife finds out. Better pay, too."

"Sounds pretty good."

"You ought to consider it. I might even be able to send some work your way."

Jake didn't know what to say. "I'll definitely think about it," he said finally.

"Here's my card," Ellis said, pulling a business card out of his shirt pocket.

They shook hands again. "Thanks. I'll let you know," Jake said as he headed back to his car.

2

Same Day: 6:10 p.m.

Jake heard the back door to the house open and close. He looked at the clock on the mantle. It was ten after six. He had meant to be working on dinner when his daughter got home. He put down the form he'd been filling out and went into the kitchen. Mary was inspecting a pot on the stove.

"What's going on, Dad? It's after six and dinner's hardly started."

Jake winced. "The chicken's in, but I didn't want to start the rice too soon." He turned on the burner under the rice. "This way, you'll have time to change before dinner. Do you want me to fix you a drink?"

"No thanks. I'll fall asleep and wake up too early. Where's Michael?"

"In his room, doing his homework."

Mary put her bags down in her corner, came over to the stove and opened the door to the oven. Jake was baking a whole chicken that he'd bought at the supermarket that afternoon.

"It takes less time if you boil it. You could have cooked it with some onions, carrots, and potatoes and had fewer dishes to clean up."

"I like the taste of baked," Jake said defensively. "So does Michael."

Mary headed into the dining room. Jake had left the light on. He saw her looking at the papers he'd been filling out.

"Dad?"

It was halfway between a question and an exclamation. Jake walked into the dining room.

"What's this?"

"Some forms I'm working on."

"What forms?"

"I'm applying for a PI's license."

"I can see that, Dad. What on earth do you need a PI's license for? You're retired."

Jake couldn't remember when he'd started letting his daughter talk to him like he was her child. Probably since she was twelve. "Retired from the Albany Police Department, yes, but that doesn't mean I'm a worn-out useless piece of crap who ought to be happy spending the rest of his life playing pinochle."

Mary looked at Jake like he had three heads and one of them just stuck its tongue out at her.

"Who said you're a worthless you-know-what?"

"No one said it, but that's how everyone makes me feel—'Heard you retired, Jake; lowered your handicap yet?' 'Heard you've retired, Mr. Barnes; planted any roses in that backyard yet?'"

"People don't know what to say, Dad. Most of them are jealous and wish they had time to play golf and work in their gardens."

"Then let them. I'm only retired because of those damn doctors and their damn tests."

"Damn tests! How about high blood pressure! How about high cholesterol! You're a walking heart attack waiting to happen." Mary put the papers down. "I can't believe you're going to become a PI, Dad. Michael and I don't want to lose you. Besides, who's going to hire you, anyway?"

Jake heard his grandson at the top of the stairs. He looked up. "Come down, Mikey. Your mom and I just are having a little conversation."

"Hi, Mom."

Michael Delany bounded down the stairs. He had his mother's dark wavy hair and fine features, but had square shoulders and the beginnings of his father's athletic build.

Mary gave him a hug and a kiss. "Got all your homework done?"

"Most of it."

"Most of it? What else have you been doing?"

"Nothing, Mom. No TV."

"Good. Go wash your hands and set the table for dinner."

Mary kept the conversation on the light and practical during dinner, which was fine with Jake. He knew she was concerned about his health, but he couldn't see himself getting any healthier sitting around the house all day with a full refrigerator begging him to open it. Besides, he had a reason for taking out the PI's license. The idea hit him while driving back home after having run into Curt Ellis. It was the perfect solution. If the Albany Police Department wasn't going to investigate Bernard Johns, having a PI's license would give him the means to do so. All he needed was a client

Peter G. Pollak

3

Saturday, April 17: 10:30 a.m.

Jake arrived at St. Peter's Episcopal Church forty-five minutes before Angela Boyer's funeral service. After parking in a nearby garage, he found a vantage point from which to observe people as they entered the church.

The current St. Peter's, a magnificent structure, which sits a few yards off Washington Avenue near the State Capitol, dates from the 1859, and is listed in the National Registry of National Landmarks. Jake, who was raised Episcopalian, had attended services at St. Peter's on many occasions.

Expecting that Bernard Johns would show up, he decided to attend Angela Boyer's funeral. He hadn't seen Johns in nearly seven years, but he picked him out easily when the dentist arrived in the company of half a dozen people about ten minutes before the service was scheduled to start. Jake was not worried that Johns would recognize him—in fact he hoped that he did, but the man never looked his way.

Remaining in the back of the church, Jake wasn't planning on confronting Johns; he merely wanted to see how he behaved during the funeral. He also wanted to observe Angela Boyer's immediate family. When they entered from the front when everyone else was seated, it was easy to pick out Angela's parents along with a brother with his wife and three small children, and a young woman, whom Jake assumed to be a sister, who came in supporting an older woman—possibly a grandmother.

The Boyers were well connected in Albany, which meant the turnout was large and included the mayor, the county executive, Assemblyman Nolan, three or four judges, and many minor officials.

During the service, Jake studied Johns and the people he was sitting with. One woman held tissues to her eyes, her shoulders shaking. Johns did not appear to display any emotion.

To investigate the circumstances of Boyer's death, he would need to interview everyone who had been on Mexican trip. Unless they had considered murder a possibility, it was unlikely that the Mexican police had conducted a thorough investigation or questioned more than a few of the club members, which meant any physical evidence that might implicate Johns—or anyone else for that matter—would be almost impossible to recover.

The first step, however, would be to confirm his suspicion that Dr. Johns was dating Boyer. If not, he'd have to admit that her death might have been the unfortunate accident as portrayed in media reports. If they were dating, however, he needed to discover the nature of their relationship. Were they were having problems? Perhaps she rejected his advances? That would fit his theory about why Johns killed Joanne Feldman and Betsy Lunsford. In either case, he needed to interview each member of the family, as well as Angela's closest women friends. The list was already getting pretty long, but that was normal for the beginning of any investigation.

While Jake could conceivably conduct an investigation without a PI's license, the license would make life a whole lot easier. It would give him greater authority when asking for interviews. More importantly, if he had a client, his time and expenses would be covered. He certainly couldn't afford to travel to Mexico on his own dime.

The logical choice for a client was Angela's father. Heathcliff Boyer was a prominent partner in one of the city's largest law firms. Money would not be a problem for Boyer, but Jake knew he would have to make a strong case that Angela had been the victim of foul play.

Dr. Johns appeared stoic during the service. Anyone disciplined enough to commit murder would not call attention to himself at his victim's funeral. As he watched Johns exit the church, Jake didn't make any effort to avoid being seen by him. If he did recognize him, Johns might not know that Jake was no longer on the police force. Therefore, Johns would have no reason to suspect that Jake's appearance at the funeral had anything to do with him—unless he was guilty, of course.

Getting a PI's license in New York State was not as easy as Jake had envisioned. The application form was long and detailed. He had to put together a portfolio documenting his education, military service, and employment history. It also asked for both work and character references. Everything had to be notarized and there was a $150 non-refundable application fee. It took more than a week for Jake to get everything ready; then he learned the State could take months to act.

He drove downtown to the Office of the Secretary of State on Washington Avenue to drop the application off in person, naïvely thinking it would get processed right away. After waiting an hour for his turn, a clerk informed him the review process could take weeks, if not months, gave Jake a receipt, and called for the next person in line.

When he got over the frustration of not knowing if or when he'd get his license, he realized there were things he could do while waiting. He'd start by organizing and reviewing the information he collected over the years on Dr. Johns' victims, beginning with the file that he had assembled on the Joanne Feldman case.

When he got home, he called his former partner, Eddie Marshall, who had retired two years ago to Florida, and asked him to send him everything that he had on the case. Next, he took a trip to an office supply store to get paper for his printer, a box of file folders with labels, pens, paperclips, and other supplies. Jake was left-handed and his writing was so far from legible that he often couldn't read something he'd written the day before. As a result, he typed all of the labels for the file folders, as well as one marked 'receipts,' which he stuck on a large envelope. He placed the receipt from the office supply store in the envelope as his first business expense.

He spent the rest of the day creating case overview documents.

When that was completed, he started putting together a list of all the people he wanted to interview, with a key that prioritized the interviews: '1' meant *Crucial*, '2' stood for *Important*, '3' was optional. He knew from past experience that he'd be adding new names to the list, as well as changing the rankings once he began the process. The first draft of his list included all fifteen of the surviving

Mexican trip participants and members of the Boyers family.

He finished by creating folders for each victim and one for Bernard Johns. His plan for the next day was to go to the library to print out every newspaper story he could find about each of the victims, as well as any he could find on Dr. Johns. Those news stories might yield additional names of people to be interviewed and possibly give him clues that would help him uncover how the murders—if they were murders—had taken place.

License or not, there was one woman he hoped would talk to him—Virginia Lunsford, the mother of the woman whose death Lieutenant Keller had prevented him from investigating.

Mary had to be at her store in the Stuyvesant Plaza Shopping Center Monday through Saturday before it opened at 10:00 am and she often stayed well past the 4:00 p.m. closing time. As a result, Jake was in charge of Mikey. This particular Saturday was the start of Little League baseball season. After breakfast, Jake took his grandson outside to get him ready for tryouts by playing pitch and catch in the driveway. He drove him to Westland Hills—the park where the Little League teams played their games— where each kid would be given a chance to impress the coaches, who later would conduct in a draft that determined which team each boy ended up on.

Jake was pleased that Mikey wanted to play baseball. He was an average kid for his age—average height, average weight, and an average attention span. Mikey might not become a star, but Jake felt it was good for kids to learn sportsmanship and teamwork at an early age.

The day began with temperatures in the low 40s and even though the sun warmed things up slightly, a brisk wind made it feel colder to the parents who stood around watching their offspring drop easy throws and boot ground balls. Mercifully, the coaches kept the boys moving. After tryouts, Jake and Mikey stopped for lunch at a nearby fast food restaurant with one of Mikey's school friends and his parents.

Jake agreed to let Mikey's friend come over that afternoon. The two boys could be counted on to play for hours with their action figures. After he got them set up in the basement rec room, he stirred some milk into heaping spoonfuls of cocoa mix and got a dish of cookies ready to take downstairs when he thought the boys might need a break.

While the boys played, he sat at the kitchen table going over the line of questioning he would take with Virginia Lunsford. Their initial phone conversation had been short. Jake had asked her if he could come by her apartment the following Monday, and reluctantly she agreed. He had just enough time to make up a list of questions before the cocoa was ready to bring downstairs.

4

Monday, April 26: 9:45 a.m.

Jake waited for the early morning rush hour to subside before heading up Interstate Route 87—known to locals as The Northway—to interview Virginia Lunsford, the mother of the woman who had been dating Dr. Bernard Johns when she fell to her death from a hiking trail near the college town of New Paltz in the fall of 1995.

Lunsford lived in a newly built apartment building near downtown Saratoga Springs. The apartment matched the building. The carpet was so plush he almost asked if he should take off his shoes and the furniture looked like the kind antique dealers would die for. Mrs. Lunsford pointed to a well-padded chair for Jake to sit in; she sat opposite him on a matching couch.

Because Mrs. Lunsford had been hesitant in allowing him to talk to her, Jake's first task was to get her to trust him. "I thought you might want to see the following materials," he said, handing her the three-ring binder that his wife Margaret had kept during his career. It contained letters of commendation, news stories of his promotions, and those when he had been the arresting officer on major cases.

"As you can see, I was a member of the Albany Police Department for thirty years," Jake said as Lunsford scrolled through the binder. "I retired earlier this year and, as I said over the phone, I was never satisfied that your daughter's death had been given as thorough an investigation as it deserved."

Virginia Lunsford looked much older than her sixty years. Her hair was a pale white and her face had a kind of sadness that Jake had seen all too often when meeting with victims' families. "I can't tell you how much it upsets me to hear you say that," she said.

"It's not that the police don't care, Mrs. Lunsford," Jake explained. "They would like nothing better than to get to the bottom of each and every case. There are only so many hours in the day."

Lunsford looked away. "I guess I'll never understand."

"When they found no evidence to the contrary, it was logical that they would draw the simplest conclusion, which was that your daughter's death was accidental."

"That's what they told me. But you don't agree?"

"Let me be very clear about this," Jake said. "I'm not saying definitively that it was not an accident, but…I don't think the possibility that she was murdered was given sufficient consideration. Now that I'm retired, I'd like to take the time to take a closer look to see if any crucial evidence might have been overlooked."

Lunsford handed him back the binder. "As I told you on the phone, Mr. Barnes, other people have offered to investigate her death for me. It's not that I can't afford it; I just don't know what good it would do."

"Mrs. Lunsford, let me be clear. I'm not asking you for a penny at this time," Jake replied. "I'll do the preliminary research at my own expense. If I find some hard evidence that her death was other than what the police concluded, then I'll come back to you with a plan to prove my theory."

"But if you don't have any evidence, I don't see why you're so interested in her case," Lunsford stated.

"That's a fair question," Jake replied. "It's because a man who was dating your daughter at the time of her death has been connected with the deaths of two other women."

Lunsford looked startled. "A man she was dating?"

"Correct."

"Do I know him? What was his name?"

"Dr. Bernard Johns."

"I don't recall her saying anything about dating a doctor, but you say this man was involved in the deaths of two other women?"

"The most recent was less than a month ago. You may have read about it," Jake said. "A woman by the name of Angela Boyer died in Mexico under mysterious circumstances. The same man who was dating your daughter at the time of her death was part of the group that accompanied Boyer to Mexico."

"So you believe this doctor killed my Betsy?"

"I don't have hard evidence at this point, Mrs. Lunsford, but the man exhibits a pattern of behavior which suggests that possibility. It's possible that he has killed three women, including your daughter . . . and, there may have been others that I don't know about."

Lunsford looked away. "I just don't know. It doesn't sound like my Betsy. She was level-headed. She wouldn't have gotten mixed up with some kind of . . . deviant."

"I can understand your doubts. All I'm asking from you today is to answer some questions. It'll only take a few minutes more."

"I don't know that I know anything that could help," Lunsford said. "I told the police all I know."

"I know you did," Jake said, "but they were operating on the assumption that your daughter's death was the result of an accident. So, shall we begin?"

"I guess so," Lunsford said finally. "I'll try my best, but I'll consult with my lawyer before I decide whether or not to hire you. I'll let him decide whether the evidence you present is sufficient."

"That's fair," Jake said. "I have no problem presenting my findings to both you and your lawyer." He took a yellow pad from his briefcase that contained the questions he planned to ask. As an experienced interviewer, Jake would let the subject's answers determine subsequent questions. The notes helped make sure he didn't forget to cover any important topics.

Jake left an hour later, having promised to keep Mrs. Lunsford informed as his investigation proceeded. He reviewed his notes while waiting for a hamburger deluxe at a *Friendly's* restaurant that he'd spotted on his way to Virginia Lunsford's apartment building.

Betsy Lunsford had been thirty-two when she went missing. She was career minded and had told her mother that she was not ready to get married or start a family. Mrs. Lunsford did not recall her daughter having mentioned dating a doctor or a man named Bernard Johns.

Mrs. Lunsford teared up when she got out a photo album to show Jake photos of Betsy growing up. The photos showed a tall attractive young woman who had participated in numerous school and community activities. She looked happy and normal, but most photos do.

"Your daughter's body was found in Dutchess County at the bottom of a hiking trail," Jake had stated near the end of the interview. "Did you know she was going hiking that weekend?"

"No, I talked to her the prior Sunday like we did every week, but she didn't tell me her plans for the following weekend."

"Was that the last time you heard from her?"

Lunsford nodded. "I'm sorry," she said as the tears fell down her face. She got up and went into the other room.

Jake sat and waited patiently.

When Mrs. Lunsford came back into the living room, Jake stood up and apologized for making her go through the pain of her daughter's death all over again.

"I don't know what good your bringing this up again is going to do," she said when she sat down on the couch. "It won't bring her back, will it?"

"No, it won't," Jake said. "However, if it was not an accident, Mrs. Lunsford, and we don't do something, the person who murdered her will be free to kill again. In fact, he may already have done so."

Virginia Lunsford indicated she would rather not continue the interview. Before he left, Jake was able to obtain a list of names of some of Betsy Lunsford's closest friends. Theoretically, he didn't need a PI's license to contact them. One had shared an apartment with Betsy for a while; others had been college friends who lived in the area. Mrs. Lunsford also gave him the name of a man Betsy had dated for several years while in her twenties. She thought he had married and moved out of the area.

Jake wanted to examine the investigation file, but would have to wait for his license to come through—assuming he'd eventually get it.

By the time he pulled into his driveway, he wasn't sure the heartburn he was feeling came from the cheeseburger he'd enjoyed at Friendly's or the thought that New York State was under no obligation to act promptly on his investigator's license, or both. Yet, he was in a good mood. The investigation had begun. From past experience, he knew these kinds of cases rarely devolved in a straight line. He was ready for whatever twists and turns the evidence would throw at him and, despite his conviction that Bernard Johns had a role in these women's deaths, he was willing to accept whatever answers he would discover at the end of the road.

5

Monday, May 3: 8:45 a.m.

Since he retired, Mondays were the toughest day of the week for Jake. Monday mornings, the week ahead loomed as a huge abyss with little to fill the hours from breakfast to dinner. His fear was that the week would go by and he would not have accomplished a thing.

He was glad to have his daughter and grandson to motivate him to get up in the morning, feeling useful by helping them get off to work and to school, and he counted walking the dog as his morning exercise, although he knew he should be doing something more strenuous. Those extra pounds were not flattering on his five-foot-ten-inch frame. But being helpful was not enough for a man who all his adult life had felt he was serving his community, meeting a need that others lacked the desire or ability to fulfill.

He was perfectly willing to do the things that needed to be done to support his daughter and grandson. But being home when Mikey got home from school, doing the grocery shopping, and cooking dinners only took up so much time.

Since he'd decided to apply for a PI license, however, things had changed. Now he had a purpose and a list of tasks that needed to get done. The problem was that he was not used to managing his own time.

When he'd been a detective working with a partner, the job imposed a structure to his weeks. For thirty years, he started each day by checking with the overnight crew for developments on his cases. Then he and his partner would plan their day, which typically meant driving to someone's office or home to try to obtain information that would enable them to make an arrest.

Working solo with no boss to report to or partner to rely on was a whole new ballgame for Jake. The previous week, he wasted several hours and put unnecessary miles on his pickup by failing to plan his activities in advance. After a frustrating few days trying to find additional information about Betsy Lunsford's death, he decided that from now on he would take Monday mornings to map out the week. He would also plan the family's evening meals for the entire week so as to reduce his trips to the grocery store.

Without a PI's license, Jake couldn't accomplish many of the things he needed to do. That meant he would have to be creative.

Although the State Police wouldn't allow him access to their file on Betsy Lunsford's death, a relative of the victim could request the final report. He called Virginia Lunsford and tried to persuade her to contact the State Police to request a copy, but she said she didn't see the point and hung up on him.

The night before, he had reached two of Betsy's women friends by phone. Neither had much useful information to contribute. The former roommate hadn't talked to Betsy for several months prior to her death. The last time she'd talked to Betsy, she'd told one of her college friends that she was going out with a couple of men she thought interesting, but wasn't in a hurry to get married.

By mid-week, Jake was becoming well known to the reference librarians at the main branch of the public library. The stories that appeared in the Albany, Troy, and Schenectady newspapers on Betsy Lunsford's death were virtually identical. The initial fact of her having gone missing had not been picked up by any of the papers. Only after her car was discovered two days after she failed to return to her hotel room did the *Poughkeepsie Journal*—the daily that covered New Paltz and the surrounding area—pick up the story. Two days after that, a police helicopter spotted her remains.

The story of her death was picked up from the *Journal* by the *Associated Press*. It was the *AP* version that ran in all three Albany area papers.

Jake added the name of the State Police investigator who had headed up the investigation to the list of people he wanted to talk to as soon as his PI's license came through.

The news stories that followed the discovery of Betsy Lunsford's body echoed the State Police's conclusion that Lunsford's death was accidental. Supporting that conclusion was the fact that she had registered by herself at the Mohonk Mountain House Hotel, a world-famous, high-end hotel located outside of the college town of New Paltz. Mohonk House offered swimming, boating, golf, and access to miles of hiking trails. It was from one of those trails that Lunsford had fallen to her death.

The *Poughkeepsie Journal* reported that a waitress at the hotel's restaurant had told investigators that a woman resembling Lunsford had eaten dinner by herself on the evening before her disappearance. Another name for the interview list.

Lunsford's body was discovered at the foot of the Devil's Way Trail—a steep and challenging hike in the best of conditions. Lunsford's backpack was found a few yards from the edge of the cliff and her locked car was still in the parking area. There was no suggestion that her death was anything but an unfortunate accident.

By the end of the week, Jake had run out of avenues to pursue on the Lunsford case; he had no choice but to switch gears and go back to the matter of Angela Boyer's death in Mexico. The first thing he decided to do was go back to the library to read up on meningitis. He wanted to be able ask intelligent questions of Dr. Smythe, the doctor who had been on the Mexico trip, as well as to be able to interpret any medical records he could obtain from the Mexican authorities. Interviewing Smythe would have to wait until he found out whether he could obtain the medical records from Mexico, and doing so would only be useful if he could find someone whose Spanish was good enough to be able to translate them for him.

Thinking it might help him see a unique pattern, Jake created timelines on heavy stock paper, blocking out the dates of each person's death and filling in what he knew about the events leading up to their deaths.

The case he knew the most about was that of Joanne Feldman, although what he knew was very sketchy. At the time of the initial investigation, he had obtained from Dr. Johns the dates when the two had met, when they had started dating as well as a timeline for the day she died— what time they'd met that morning and approximately the time when she "fell" over the edge.

For Boyer, he needed to learn the dates for the Mexico trip, including when they'd arrived at the resort where she died, what time they'd discovered that she was ill, and so forth.

For Lunsford, he had the date of her last conversation with her mother and the date her body was discovered. What he lacked was information about Bernard Johns' whereabouts during that time period. Trying to obtain that nearly four years later would definitely be a challenge.

The first Monday in May, Jake saw that he had no more than two days' worth of research to keep him busy. A week later, he sat in front of a blank sheet of paper. There was virtually nothing he didn't know that he could find out at this point. He got up and started to dial Virginia Lunsford's phone number to try again to get her to request the coroner's report, but hung up the phone before she answered. He didn't know what he could say that would be more convincing than what he'd already said to her. *Now what?*

Jake took Benji out for a long walk. Sweating by the time he got back to the house, he was proud of himself when he drank two glasses of water instead of pouring himself another cup of coffee. He wouldn't eat lunch until twelve thirty, plus he had given up doughnuts. With nothing else to do, he could go to the store for some groceries, but knew he'd be tempted to buy something sweet if he went before lunch.

Cops typically don't have friends outside of work. When they socialize, it is with other cops and their families. Some of Jake's cop friends had retired and left the area; others were still on the job. He thought of calling Curt Ellis. Maybe he'd do that later.

Jake's biggest regret in life was that he and Margaret had not been able to have more children. Margaret had miscarried twice before Mary was born and then once again afterwards. She finally told Jake she couldn't go through it again. They had discussed adopting, but, given Jake's career, the fact that he often worked late into the evening, he was afraid he couldn't be the kind of father an adopted child would need. He wasn't a reader and didn't have any hobbies. He had tried golf a few times, but hadn't fallen in love with it. What other sport could an overweight fifty-five-year-old man get into?

He was at a dead end and didn't have a plan B.

6

Wednesday, June 2: 10:00 a.m.

Two weeks went by and nothing changed—no PI license, no unturned stones waiting to be looked under. Jake puttered around the house. He straightened up the tools in his garage, mowed the lawn, and watched parts of a lot of old movies on TV. He even moved the boxes in the basement that were sitting on the weight-lifting bench he hadn't used in five years and started the routine he had done every other day for years. Knowing he couldn't start with the same weights he'd been able to lift in the past, he set up the weights twenty pounds lighter and did fewer sets, but with all that, there were still too many hours in the day with nothing for him to do.

Mary sat down with him one night to go over plans for the summer. In late July, Mikey would spend a couple of weeks with his father, who planned to take him to Michigan where his family owned a cabin on a lake. Otherwise, the ten-year-old would go to two sports day camps—one for baseball and one for basketball. Mary asked Jake if he would drop him off and pick him up in the afternoon. Mary wanted to take a couple of weeks off and was thinking about doing a trip with Mikey to Maine in August. When she asked Jake what he'd like to do that summer, he said he hadn't thought about it.

Later that day, sitting on his front porch, Jake realized he didn't have anything he looked forward to doing. Maybe it wasn't too late to start a vegetable garden.

At 9:00 a.m. on the second Tuesday in June, Jake stood in front of the cordless telephone that hung on the wall in the kitchen, rehearsing.

He was still breathing heavily from his walk with his grandson's dog. He tried to convince himself that walking Benji twice a day meant he was getting the exercise his doctor recommended. He didn't feel out of breath as often now as he had when he started walking the dog right after Mary and Michael moved into his house, but he'd taken the long route that morning and felt it.

Yet, Jake knew the sweat running down his sides was from nervousness, not the walk.

Finally, he picked up the phone and walked into the living room where the phone number he wanted to call was written in large block numbers on a yellow pad.

He hesitated, then, like a swimmer who knows he's in for a shock when he hits the cold water, he dialed the number. The phone was picked up on the second ring.

"Hartfield, Boyer and Leatherberry. May I help you?"

"Yes, you may. My name is Jake Barnes. I'd like to speak to Mr. Boyer."

"May I tell him what it's about?"

Jake hesitated, not having anticipated the question. "I'd rather not say."

"May I say where you're calling from?"

"It's a personal call."

"Certainly. You said your name is Jack Barnes?"

"Jake, not Jack. Actually, it's Robert. Robert Barnes."

"Hold on, please."

The phone went to classical music as the receptionist put him on hold.

Jake looked down at his legal pad where he'd written a few keywords to remind him what he'd planned to say when Mr. Boyer came on the line.

"Mr. Barnes." It was the receptionist. "Mr. Boyer is in a meeting right now. He asked me to take down your information and ask if you're calling to engage him in a legal matter."

"Yes. Good. I'd like to set up an appointment...at his office, of course."

"Of course. Let me check his schedule." There was a pause. "How would next Wednesday at three thirty be?"

"You have nothing earlier?"

"No, I'm afraid Mr. Boyer has quite a busy schedule. You're fortunate that spot is open. We had a cancellation."

"Well then, I'll take next Wednesday at three-thirty." He hung up the phone. "All right!" he said out loud.

Next to the weeks he'd spent watching his wife die, the past three weeks had been the worst weeks of his life. He had fallen off the diet wagon, he wasn't getting enough exercise, and he couldn't think of a thing he looked forward to doing except perhaps going fishing with Mikey when school was over. Then one day, there it was—an envelope from the Secretary of State's office.

Before he opened it, he had a moment where he thought perhaps the fact that he was hearing from them so soon meant his application for a PI's license had been rejected. He decided there was no way he would accept a denial. There had to be an appeals process. He'd appeal, and, if they wanted more information, he'd get it for them. *He wasn't going to give up. He would accept setbacks, but no defeats.* After taking a deep breath, he opened the envelope. He had to read the certificate three times before it registered that his application had been accepted. He was in the game.

Jake entered the State Street building in downtown Albany where Hartfield, Boyer and Leatherberry had their offices a few minutes before three-thirty the following Wednesday. He planned to get there earlier, but had lost track of time going over his notes and then had trouble finding a parking space. He ended up having to park in a garage in back of the Omni Hotel.

Jake was dressed in the suit and tie Margaret had helped him pick out many years ago at a men's store in the mall. The pants waist was tight, as was the neck on the white shirt that had been hanging in his closet for months, still in its plastic bag from the dry cleaner. The temperature outside was in the mid 70s. He was sweating by the time he reached the entrance to the building from the heat and from the fear that he would be tossed out on his ear when Heathcliff Boyer discovered that he was not there to engage him on a legal matter but instead to ask Angela Boyer's father to hire him instead.

One of Albany's top law firms, Hartfield, Boyer and Leatherberry was the kind of firm that doesn't mess around with your typical real estate closing or uncontested divorce. The librarian at the main branch of the public library on Washington Avenue helped Jake learn about Boyer from newspaper stories, as well as from an edition of *Who's Who in New York State*. Boyer was a graduate of Syracuse University and had joined the law firm his father had helped found right out of Albany Law School. He was a big contributor to the local hospital and other charitable organizations. Angela had been the middle of his three children.

Checking the directory in the lobby on the first floor, Jake saw that the firm occupied the twenty-second and twenty-third floors. As he got off the elevator, there was a large reception desk directly in front of him and two sets of doors barring access to the back offices. The firm's name was mounted on the wall behind the receptionist in large golden letters on a wooden background.

Jake announced himself and was told to take a seat. He pawed through a stack of magazines and was surprised to find, in addition to the *Wall Street Journal*, *Forbes* and *Travel & Leisure*, the latest *Sports Illustrated*. He caught himself almost lost in an article about the pro basketball playoffs. *Don't forget why you're here*. He put down the magazine and pulled out the sheet of paper from his jacket pocket that contained his talking points. He had spent several hours writing word for word how he wanted to present his case for Boyer to hire him to investigate his daughter's death, then condensed his pitch into several short phrases that introduced the key arguments he wanted to make.

As he waited, he became aware of a loud conversation. The door to the back offices was partially opened, but no one came out.

"Admit it! You don't care what she would have wanted!"

It was a woman's voice. Jake couldn't hear the response.

"I'm going," the woman said. "I don't know why I even came here. Your clients are more important to you than your own children."

"Chloe. That's uncalled for."

A young woman with wild hair came stamping out the door and headed for the elevator.

"What are you looking at?" she said to Jake as she walked by.

"Sorry, Miss." He looked over at the secretary, who was trying to mind her own business, then realized he'd seen the woman someplace. It was at Angela Boyer's funeral—that must be her younger sister. She was standing with her back to him waiting for the elevator. It finally came. Ten minutes later, a woman came out to the reception area.

"Mr. Barnes?"

"That's me."

"Mr. Boyer will see you now."

Jake got up and followed the woman into the inner sanctum of HB&L.

Heathcliff Boyer was of medium height and build. He looked the part of successful lawyer in his expensive gray suit, white shirt, and maroon tie. He had a full head of hair and perfect white teeth. Boyer welcomed Jake, shook his hand, and offered him a seat on the leather couch in his large office, then sat in a red leather chair opposite the couch.

"What brings you to Hartfield, Boyer and Leatherberry, Mr. Barnes? Before you answer, I would like to know why you asked specifically to meet with me. I should warn you that my rates are very high. However, we have some very talented younger associates who may be able to assist you."

Jake pulled one of the business cards he had printed at the quick print store at Crossgates Mall out of his shirt pocket and handed it to Boyer. The clerk had helped Jake lay out the design.

"I'm actually not here to hire you, Mr. Boyer. I'm here to ask you to hire me."

"Hire you? To do what?"

"To investigate your daughter's death."

Boyer's face got red. "See here. What's the meaning of this?"

"Please, let me explain," Jake said quickly. "I recently retired from the Albany Police Department as Detective First Class. Some years ago, I investigated the untimely deaths of two area women. The man I believe had something to do with those deaths was on the Mexican trip with your daughter."

"Are you talking about Dr. Smythe? I already had someone look into it. Dr. Smythe did everything he could to save Angela's life. He was devastated by her death."

"No, I'm not referring to Dr. Smythe. I hesitate to give you the person's name because in part because I do not have proof that this individual—"

"Mr. Bernard, or whomever you are—"

"Barnes. Robert Barnes."

"Barnes, then. The point is that my daughter died of the sudden onset of spinal meningitis. There's no reason to think that it was anything except for tragic bad luck to contract that disease so far from modern medical facilities."

"I understand, and again, I want to restate that I do not have any concrete evidence. However, there are strong reasons that someone should investigate further into what happened. Wouldn't you like to know one hundred percent for certain that everything happened as you've been told?"

"Our insurance company has already conducted a thorough investigation. If they came up with any evidence that this was anything other than what has been reported, they would have contacted the appropriate authorities."

"If they knew what to look for."

Peter G. Pollak

"What are you saying? That her death was not an accident?"

"I'm saying someone ought to investigate whether an individual on that trip contributed to her death in some way."

"Based on what--something that happened in the past? Was this person ever arrested or convicted?"

Jake hesitated. "No."

"Neither?"

"Neither."

Boyer raised his eyebrows. Jake could see that the man was beginning to lose his patience. "Mr. Barnes. Do you have a license as a private investigator?"

"Yes, I do."

"May I see it?"

"I didn't think to bring it with me, but I can…"

"Never mind. I know there are people who prey on those who have recently suffered from a loss. I hope you're not one of those people."

"No. I certainly am not—"

Boyer interrupted. "And, I'll have you know, I'm not the kind of person who can be taken advantage of."

"That certainly wasn't my intention."

"Nevertheless, I am going to have to say 'no' to hiring you. If the insurance investigation raised unanswered questions and you had information that seemed pertinent, that would be another matter. I have your business card and will contact you if anything changes. Now, I have other business that I must attend to. You'll excuse me." As he stood up, after hesitating for a moment, Boyer extended his hand.

Jake shook his hand and started to leave the office. "Mr. Boyer. Just let me say one final thing. It was not easy for me to come here today. I only did so because I sincerely

46

believe that a local individual has successfully gotten away with murdering two women and may have had a hand in your daughter's death. I hope that is not the case, but there's only one way to find out."

"I appreciate your sincerity, Mr. Barnes, and as I said, I will contact you if I feel there is anything you can do for us. Now, good day."

Peter G. Pollak

7

Thursday, June 3: 11:45 a.m.

"What a nice surprise," Mary Delany said, seeing her father enter her dress shop in Stuyvesant Plaza in uptown Albany.

"I thought I'd stop by and take you out to lunch," Jake said, surveying the store, which he had not visited for several months. He never understood why she crowded the narrow store with so many racks of clothes. How can shoppers find what they are looking for?

"I wish you had called, Dad," Mary said. "I'm here all by myself. Caroline had a doctor's appointment and won't be back until two."

Jake frowned. "You can't close the shop for a while?"

"No! Lunch is a time when a lot of professional women stop by. In fact, I've got a customer in the dressing room."

"Okay," Jake said. "I understand." While he admired his daughter's drive, he didn't understand why she couldn't work for a large company instead of trying to make a go of it on her own. She had used the money she'd obtained from her divorce to buy out the previous owner. It seemed too demanding and risky.

"Was there something in particular that you wanted to talk to me about?" Mary asked.

"I just thought I'd take my daughter out to lunch," Jake replied. "I even dressed up."

They both laughed. Jake was not known as a dresser and lately he'd paid less attention to his clothes than ever. Instead of suits when he had to dress professionally, he wore a plaid sports jacket with a white dress shirt, a subdued blue-striped tie, khaki pants, and comfortable brown shoes.

"Excuse me a minute, Dad," Mary said, turning and heading back into the dressing room area.

Jake didn't know what to do with himself while he waited. He had suggested that Mary add a couple of chairs for the men who might come into the store with their wives and girlfriends, but she told him that men rarely came into her store these days. Modern women shopped on their own without their men tagging along.

Mary really did seem to be busy. He thought about leaving, but didn't want her to think he was upset that she wasn't available for lunch. He actually did have an agenda. He wanted to try to explain why he was pursuing Dr. Johns and hoped discussing it over lunch in public would be easier than his attempts to do so at home in the evening with Mikey close by.

Of course, having been turned down by Heathcliff Boyer, it looked like all his prior work had been for naught. It would be very difficult to do the job right without a paying client. While he could interview people in Albany, he couldn't afford a trip to Mexico to talk to the authorities there. Chances were, he would never be able to obtain the necessary proof to convince Art Keller of Johns' guilt. Just when he thought things were looking up, he had to face the possibility that someone else would have to make the connection between Johns and yet another victim. Jake hated to think that he was at a dead end.

Mary came out with her customer who took one look at Jake and stepped back with a startled look on her face.

"You," the woman said. "Didn't I see you in my father's office yesterday?"

It was Angela Boyer's sister.

"If your father is Heathcliff Boyer, the answer is yes," Jake said.

"Are you following me? Did my father put you up to this?" She was clearly angry, which was upsetting Mary as well.

"No, I only met your father for the first time yesterday."

"Then what are you doing here?" the woman demanded.

"Actually, I'm visiting my daughter," Jake replied, nodding in his daughter's direction. "My name is Jake Barnes and this is my daughter, Mary Delany."

The woman turned to look at Mary and then looked back at Jake. "I never would have guessed," she said. "I'm sorry if I jumped on you, but I wouldn't put it past my father to hire someone to follow me."

Jake hesitated, not certain if he should tell her the reason for having contacted her father. "I was sorry to read about your sister's death."

The woman's face fell. She seemed about to cry.

"I'm sorry. I don't mean to upset you," Jake mumbled.

The woman took a tissue out of her pocket and wiped her eyes. "Did you know Angela?" she asked.

"No, I never had the pleasure," he replied.

"I thought I saw you at the funeral."

"I was there. It's hard to explain," Jake said.

"Oh?" the woman said. "Please try."

"Yes, please do," chimed in his daughter.

"I don't want to alarm you, Miss Boyer—"

"My name's Chloe," the woman interrupted.

"Fine. As I was saying, Chloe, I don't want to alarm you, but there are unanswered questions about your sister's death."

Chloe was taken aback. "What kind of questions?"

"For one, why did it take so long for the people she was with to notice that she was seriously ill, and why, with two people in the group with medical training, did it take so long for them to get help? I thought your father might be interested in having someone look for some answers."

"You said two people with medical training. Dr. Smythe is one, but who was the second person?"

"Bernard Johns—the dentist."

"Well, you really can't count him, can you?"

"I would. Dentists these days receive more basic medical training than you'd expect," Jake said.

"So the two of them should have recognized Angela's illness and done something in time to save her life? Is that what you're saying?" Chloe asked.

"That's one issue, but I haven't interviewed everyone on the trip and I don't have access to the medical or police reports. Therefore, I can't say for certain that your sister's death was anything but terrible bad luck."

Chloe raised an eyebrow. "That seems pretty flimsy to me."

"I agree," Mary piped in.

Jake hesitated, but then decided something else needed to be said. "There's one more fact that strongly suggests the need to look further."

"What's that?" Chloe asked.

"Dr. Bernard Johns' name has come up in the investigation of two other unusual deaths—both women he was dating at the time."

Chloe looked startled. "Two other women? My gosh! What are you saying, Mr. Barnes?"

"I'm saying that someone ought to investigate to make sure foul play was not involved in your sister's death. That's what I went to see your father about."

"And what did he say?" Chloe asked.

"He said that nothing had come up in the insurance investigation and as far as he was concerned there was nothing to investigate."

Chloe stood thinking for a minute. Just then, two women came into the shop. Mary excused herself.

Jake decided to take a chance on prolonging the conversation. "I couldn't help but hear that you were having an argument with your father yesterday. May I ask, was it about Angela's death?

"It's a long story," Chloe said.

"Maybe we could talk someplace more private. There's a Starbucks a few doors down."

"Too noisy. We could go to Spinelli's."

Spinelli's was a fancy restaurant located in the Plaza that specialized in crepes and salads with sun-dried tomatoes.

"Fine with me," Jake said.

Chloe went back into the changing room to change. While he waited, Jake hoped to have a word with his daughter, but she was busy helping customers.

When Chloe came out of the dressing room, she returned the dresses that she had tried on to the rack and indicated she was ready to join him. While holding the front door for Chloe Boyer, Jake looked back to see if his daughter noticed that he was leaving. She had a stern look on her face. He'd be getting an earful later.

Spinelli's Café was not the kind of restaurant Jake was used to frequenting. Reading the menu, he saw that they specialized in lunches with small portions with fancy deserts and their coffees cost as much as Starbucks' priciest. He couldn't find anything on the menu that resembled a ham on rye, so he settled for chicken salad wrap and a cup of coffee. Chloe ordered a diet soda.

"So, you and your father don't see eye to eye?" Jake asked after the waitress had taken their order.

"I'm too independent and hang around people he wouldn't be seen dead with," Chloe admitted.

"You're the youngest, right?"

Chloe nodded, looking down at her hands. Jake felt bad for constantly reminding her of her sister's death.

"What were you and your father arguing about, if I may ask?"

"He invited that dentist fellow to a ceremony we're having at St. Rose. My parents are donating one million dollars to the college in Angela's name. I told him that Dr. Johns was a creep. My father wouldn't listen."

"So Bernard Johns was dating your sister?"

"Yes. She had gone out with him for about six or seven months."

"And why do you think he's a creep?" Jake asked.

"You said as much yourself, didn't you?" Chloe replied. "You said two women that he had been dating died strange deaths."

"I did, but I'm curious as to why you consider him a creep?"

Chloe wrinkled her nose. "I didn't like him the first time I met him. I thought Angela was too good for him. She was smart, sophisticated, and very energetic. He didn't seem to bring that much to the party. He was content just to be seen with her."

"Did she have feelings for him?"

"She might have been attracted to him at first. He must be ten years older, but he does keep himself in decent shape. They enjoyed similar things, but after a while I think she came to agree with me. He never expressed strong opinions about anything. She had to initiate everything—what restaurant to eat at, what movie to see. It gets tiresome being the one who decides everything."

The waitress interrupted the conversation by bringing their drinks. Jake, who had ordered a plain coffee, smelled some flavoring in the cup that was placed in front of him. He added some cream and a level spoon of sugar—he used to put in two—stirred it and sipped. Flavored coffee must be the new plain.

"Tell me more about Angela," Jake said. "From the picture I saw in the paper, she was quite attractive. Why did she belong to a single's club?"

"Initially she went because a girlfriend asked her to go with her. She enjoyed the activities and I guess she found it easier to meet men that way. She didn't frequent clubs like I do and had exhausted the eligible men she met through her job."

"The paper said she was a physical therapist."

"That's right. My father wanted her to go law school or become a CPA, but she enjoyed sports and wanted to help people with injuries. She worked out of a small medical practice. The rest of the time she volunteered and took trips with that damn club."

The waitress brought Jake his wrap. Chloe decided she'd eat something and made the waitress wait while she perused the menu before deciding to have a small salad with dressing on the side.

"What kind of health was Angela in?" Jake asked after the waitress left.

"She was in very good health. In addition to hiking, skiing, and swimming, she was a good tennis player. She was the women's tennis champion at our country club three years running. She did have diabetes, but she kept it under control by watching her diet and she was extremely diligent in checking her blood sugar."

"Here's why I ask," Jake said. "I have done some research on meningitis. The dangerous kind is bacterial meningitis. That's probably what Angela had. In order to catch it, however, she would have had to come into close contact with someone who was already infected with the disease. To my knowledge, none of the other people in the singles club has shown any symptoms. That raises the question of how the disease was transmitted to her."

Chloe took that all in. "Do you have a theory?" she asked.

"Not yet, but it's possible, by talking to the people who were on the trip, that I can uncover some clue as to how she contracted the disease."

Chloe nodded.

"I would also like to talk to public health officials in Mexico to find out if other cases have been reported in that region. If not, then other possibilities have to be considered."

"Wouldn't the insurance department do all that?" Chloe asked.

"Only if they were considering the possibility that someone infected her intentionally would they try to rule out all other forms of contact. That's why I believe your father should hire someone. It doesn't have to be me, but someone should do a thorough investigation."

"He won't do it," Chloe said. "He loved Angela dearly—probably more than Mark or myself—but he's stubborn."

"Mark's your brother?"

Chloe nodded. Jake took another bite of the wrap. "I'm sorry to have brought all this up," he said. "I'm only upsetting you and it appears you'll never get a satisfactory answer."

Chloe was silent. She nibbled at her salad. "Couldn't they have done something . . . to save her, I mean?"

"Possibly . . . if it had been diagnosed sooner and she'd been given the right antibiotic. I'm sure the insurance people talked to Dr. Smythe, but I'd like to know if they asked him why no one noticed how sick Angela was feeling until it was too late."

"Wasn't that his job?"

"I don't know that he was on the trip in a professional capacity. But, if someone had pointed out that Angela had a high fever, was vomiting and felt weak, I assume he would have looked into it. My guess is that she was too weak to get out of bed and Dr. Smythe was not told she was sick until it was too late."

Chloe thought for a moment. "But shouldn't someone else in the group have noticed—even if she wasn't able to ask for help herself?"

"You're absolutely correct," Jake said. "That's why all of the people on the trip should be interviewed."

Chloe leaned back and dabbed her eyes with her napkin. "Poor Angie," she said, unable to hold back the tears. Jake could think of nothing appropriate to say, so he sat and waited. Chloe excused herself and headed toward the restrooms.

"I'm sorry," she said, back at the table ten minutes later.

"There's nothing to apologize for," Jake stated.

"I loved my sister too much not to know the truth."

"Maybe your father will listen to you."

"No, I'm pretty sure he won't. There is an alternative, however," she said.

"What's that?"

"My grandmother. She was totally devastated by Angie's death and she listens to me. I'll talk to her, but you need to tell me how much an investigation would cost."

"I worked up some figures for your father. I have the information in my car. I'm parked near my daughter's store."

They walked back across the parking lot, saying very little. Jake had left his briefcase in the car after the unsuccessful meeting with Heathcliff Boyer. He gave Chloe the two-page financial estimate that he'd drawn up. It was the first time that he'd put together a budget for a private investigation and he'd taken a lot of time with it, arguing with himself over the numbers and changing them several times.

He estimated the investigation would take at least two months. He decided to charge $250/day for his time. The trip to Mexico, if necessary, would cost around $3,000. He was asking for $5,000 in advance, with a promise to submit a detailed report of his time and expenses at the end of the investigation.

Chloe didn't seem at all put off by the numbers. She promised to get back to him after talking to her grandmother.

8

Same Day: 8:30 p.m.

That night, after Mary put her son to bed, she came downstairs and found her father on the couch in the den watching a basketball game.

"Dad. Is this a good time to talk?" she inquired.

"Sure," Jake replied. He had mentioned when she got home that they should talk. He turned off the TV. "About today," he started, "I hope I didn't cost you a sale."

Mary sat down on a chair. Jake thought she looked a bit tired. "I'm not worried about that," she said. "She'll be back."

"Good," he said. "Glad to hear that."

"So what did the two of you talk about?"

"I gave her a brief rundown of why I thought an investigation into her sister's death was warranted."

"To what end, Dad?"

"First off, I didn't want to continue the conversation in your store. That wouldn't have been fair to you or your customers."

"Thank you."

Jake smiled. "But she wanted to know why I felt an investigation is needed. So, I told her."

"Is she going to talk to her father?"

"She doesn't feel her talking to him will do much good. She's going to talk to her grandmother instead. Apparently she was very close to Angela and was very upset at her death. Chloe brought it up. I didn't encourage her, but I didn't discourage her either."

"So, help me understand what's motivating you, Dad. I know you suspect this dentist had something to do with it, but it happened in Mexico. Doesn't it require someone with the right kind of authority to get answers?"

Jake nodded. "That very well may be, Mary, and I'm not saying I can do this alone, but since Art Keller isn't going to do anything unless the culprit walks into the station house and says he wants to confess, someone has to compile the evidence and, if he's guilty, put a stop to this guy."

"And you think you can do that?"

"I've only been retired for four months. I didn't forget everything I learned in thirty years of police work."

"Of course not," Mary replied. "I'm not saying that, but I guess I'm still not sure why you can't put this police business to bed. You gave it the best years of your life. You should be able to enjoy yourself and not worry about murderers."

"That's the point, Mary. Police work is what I do best. It's who I am and I'm good at it, or at least I used to be."

"But this dentist guy—this is more than just another case to you, right?"

"Okay. I admit it. I guess it bothered me that I couldn't pin that woman's death on him seven years ago. We should have been able to find the hole in his story, but we didn't.

Then, a few years later, another woman who was dating Dr. Johns goes off a cliff in Dutchess County. I thought we ought to look into it, but I couldn't convince Keller. The State Police declared it an accident and we had enough other unsolved cases on the board."

"What if he's innocent?"

"I don't think he is, but if it turns out that I can't make a case, I'll back off."

Mary nodded.

"I guess I never really told you why I became a cop," Jake said after a minute. "Your mother always said it was because I wasn't smart enough to do anything else, but, of course, she was expressing in her own way the frustration that wives of cops put up with."

"She never let it get to her, did she?"

"Well, she came close a couple of times," Jake said. "Like when I got shot back in eighty-three. But she was a trooper. I really miss her."

Mary looked down. "Me too."

Jake reached over to pat his daughter's hand on the arm of the chair in which she was sitting.

"So, why did you?"

"Why did I what?"

"Become a cop?"

"Oh, sorry. I lost track of what we were talking about for a minute there. When I was a kid, I saw a cop rescue a man who was trapped in a car that had been blind-sided at an intersection. Cars didn't have seat belts in those days or gas tanks that didn't blow up. This cop, who happened to live next door to us, must have heard the crash. He came out of his house half-dressed and was able to get the guy out of the car minutes before the gasoline, which was leaking from the tank, caught on fire and blew the car up. I was about ten at the time."

Mary nodded. "That's quite a story.

"By the way, the man in the car. That was your grandfather."

"Grandpa Walter."

Jake nodded. "Later, this same cop—Andrews, I think his name was—came to our school. I raised my hand and asked him if he was ever scared. He said—and I remember his exact words—he said 'helping people was his job and he didn't have time to be scared.'"

"That did it for me. After I did my tour in the Army, I applied to the Police Academy and the rest, as they say, is history."

The rest of the week and the weekend dragged. Jake kept arguing with himself about whether he could conduct a thorough enough investigation without a paying client. There was a lot he could do in Albany, and if it turned out that he needed to go to Mexico, well, he'd have to cross that bridge when he got to it.

Monday he was back at the library researching Dr. Johns—where he went to school, the associations he belonged to, anything he could find. There were numerous small mentions in the newspaper of his having attended such-and-such a seminar or having completed such-and-such a course. The guy got around.

Tuesday morning, he got a phone call from Chloe Boyer. She asked him to meet her at twelve thirty the next day at Spinelli's.

Jake was tempted to stop to pick up a ham and cheese on rye on the way there, but resisted. Chloe wasn't there when he arrived, so he sat down and ordered a plain coffee.

She arrived fifteen minutes late without bothering to apologize. After she'd ordered a salad and a diet soda, she sat there, seemingly hesitant about something.

"Well," Jake said finally. "Why are we here?"

"My grandmother said it is up to me," Chloe admitted. "I'm trying to decide if I should hire you or find someone else."

"Someone else?"

"You know. Someone who inspires more confidence."

Jake tried not to take the comment personally. He loosened his tie. "Never judge a book by its cover."

"I guess you're right, but tell me again why we should hire you."

"I spent thirty years on the Albany Police Department, Ms. Boyer," Jake said, trying not to sound like he was annoyed at having to give his resume to a twenty-something-year-old party girl. "In the course of the investigation of the death of a woman that Bernard Johns had been dating, I began to suspect that Dr. Johns was not telling the whole story, but I was unable to prove otherwise. And, there's a good possibility that he was responsible in some way for your sister's death. You can try to find another private detective to take the case, but that person would have to spend weeks, if not months, to catch up to where I am today. I have a plan and I am ready to start today." He paused to let that sink in. "So," he asked, "what's it to be? Do you want me to investigate your sister's death or not?"

"You don't have to get angry," Chloe said.

"I'm not angry, Ms. Boyer. I just want you to understand that this is not just another job for me. I believe that Bernard Johns may be responsible for the deaths of three women, one being your sister. All three died in the prime of life. If he is guilty and no one stops him, there'll be another funeral down the road. You can count on it."

Chloe nodded. She picked at her salad. "Okay. You're right. You're the one who should investigate, but . . ."

"But what?"

"There is one condition."

Jake arched an eyebrow. "And that is?"

Chloe hesitated, and then blurted it out. "I want you to hire me as your assistant . . . I mean, you don't have to pay me. You just have to include me . . .well . . . sort of."

Jake shook his head, but didn't say anything for a second. He took a deep breath. "Hire you to do what exactly?"

"Investigate."

"And do you have some experience with murder investigations?"

Chloe shook her head. "I can learn. I'm smart. I know how to use a computer—better than you, I'll bet."

"Probably true," he admitted, "but I'm not sure I understand what you're asking of me."

"I just don't want to hang out with my friends and pretend everything's normal while you're investigating Angela's death. I want to help you solve it."

Jake nodded. "I understand how you feel, but a murder investigation is neither fun nor easy. In fact, it can be very dangerous to one's health if you don't know what you're doing."

She nodded. "I can help. I really can."

He saw something in her face that he hadn't seen before. The gee-whiz-look-at-me demeanor was gone. Perhaps for the first time in her adult life Chloe Boyer sounded serious. He took a deep breath and made a rash decision. "Okay. I'll take you on as my assistant. But I also have one condition."

"What's that?" Chloe said, allowing a shy smile to break out on her face.

"That you do what I ask you to do and that you don't do anything that I don't ask you to do without checking with me first."

Chloe nodded.

"Say it, please."

"I agree," she said, nodding her head.

He sighed. "Okay, then; you're hired."

Chloe reached into her purse, took out an envelope and pushed it across the table.

Jake opened the envelope. Inside was a check for $5,000 made out to Robert J. Barnes. He put it back in the envelope and stuffed it into his jacket.

"When do we start?" Chloe asked.

"Right now. Here's what I want you to do. Go home and make up a list of your sister's closest women friends, as well as every man she dated since she was a teenager. Find their current addresses and phone numbers. Call me when you have it ready. And, listen, now. This is important. Don't tell anyone—not even your grandmother—the specifics of what we're doing: not who we're investigating nor what anyone tells us. If she or anyone else in your family asks, say they have to talk to me. Got it?"

She nodded. "What are you going to do now?"

"I've got a long list of people I need to interview, starting with the people who were on the Mexico trip. We'll go over what we've learned once we get through this first round of interviews and take it from there."

"Do you want to meet some of the people who were on the Mexico trip before you interview them?"

"What do you mean?" Jake asked.

"The singles club is having a networking event to raise money for Habitat for Humanity in Angela's name."

"When is it?"

"Tomorrow night. They asked me if I'd come and say a few words about why the family picked Habitat as Angela's charity."

"Are you going?"

Chloe nodded.

"I'll have to think about whether it would be wise for me to go," Jake said. "I'll call you tomorrow to let you know."

"See! I can be of help," Chloe said with a shy grin.

"Keep on proving it," Jake said. He got up and threw a $10 bill on the table. "Later," he said, heading for the exit.

Jake told himself that he was crazy to agree to Chloe Boyer's demand, but when he reached the sidewalk, he stopped, took a deep breath, and smiled. Despite having to watch out for a twenty-something party girl, he was in business. *Look out, Dr. Johns. Here I come.*

9

Thursday, June 10: 5:35 p.m.

Jake was surprised to find himself feeling nervous as he walked up to the entrance to the restaurant where the Albany Singles Club was holding a networking event to raise money for Habitat for Humanity in Angela Boyer's memory. He had been struggling over whether or not to tell the people he met that evening that he was conducting an investigation into Boyer's death. He finally made his decision on the drive downtown that he would have to do tell them about the investigation, even though he wasn't entirely comfortable doing so. If he didn't tell people, however, they would be right not to trust him when he contacted them later for interviews. The flipside was if he told them now, it would give advance warning to anyone who might have information she or he wanted to withhold. That person might concoct a lie or not agree to speak to him, but that was a risk he would have to take. In the final analysis, going to the event might turn out to be a good thing. At minimum, it would give him another chance to observe Bernard Johns, assuming he showed.

The event was scheduled from five-thirty to seven-thirty. Jake saw Dr. Johns enter a few minutes after he arrived. Chloe, on the other hand, wasn't there yet. That didn't surprise him. After he filled a plate with veggies and onion dip and poured himself a diet soda, he looked for a group of people to introduce himself to. He noticed two women sitting at a table where there was an empty chair. He asked if the chair was taken. After they invited him to join them, he introduced himself and asked if either had known Angela.

"We both did," stated the woman whose nametag identified her as Ellen. The other woman, whose nametag read 'Marlene,' nodded in agreement.

"Were either of you on the Mexican trip?" Jake asked.

"Both of us were," Ellen replied.

"That must have been awful … and terrifying," Jake ventured.

Ellen nodded. "It was that and more."

"Words can't describe how upset we both were . . . and still are," Marlene stated.

"I guess I'll learn the gruesome details soon enough," Jake said.

"Why's that?" Ellen inquired.

"I've been hired by the family to conduct an investigation."

"What kind of investigation?" Marlene asked.

"There are some unanswered questions about what happened."

"I don't think there's much to find," Ellen said.

"Why's that?"

"One day she was feeling under the weather and the next day she was . . . you know."

"And what good will an investigation do?" Marlene asked. "It won't bring her back."

"No, of course not," he replied. "But it's normal in situations like this for the family to want to know exactly what took place."

"Maybe they're looking to sue someone," Ellen suggested to her friend.

"Not necessarily."

Ellen gave him a friendly smile. "Well, good luck."

"Thanks," Jake replied. "Since both of you were on the trip, I'd like to contact each of you to set up a time to talk."

"I don't see what good that would do," Ellen said. Marlene nodded her agreement.

"I plan on talking to everyone who was on the trip. If there's nothing to add to what they already know, that in itself will help ease the family's concerns. So, would it be okay if I call you?"

"I guess so," Ellen said, "but I'm telling you now, we don't know anything that hasn't already been reported."

Jake thanked the women and was about to get up to refill his plate when a woman started banging on her glass, asking for everyone's attention. She introduced herself as the president of the club, thanked everyone for attending and for their donations. She started to go over the dates for upcoming events when Chloe Boyer made her entrance. The club president motioned for Chloe to join her and then introduced her to the group.

Chloe stumbled over her brief remarks. The emotion of the moment seemingly caught her off-guard.

As the event resumed, Jake wandered around the room, introducing himself to people, asking if they knew Angela and were on the trip. He tried to keep himself positioned where he could observe Bernard Johns. The dentist was making no effort to maintain a solemn demeanor. He was at the center of a group of five or six people who were enjoying a story he was telling with winks and chuckles. Jake made mental note of each person in the group, but made no attempt to approach them.

As per Jake's instructions, Chloe left after half an hour without having talked to him. He started for the exit a while later when one of the women he'd met earlier intercepted him. "Mr. Barnes. There are some people who'd like to meet you."

"Oh?"

"Over here." Ellen led him to the group that included Marlene and Dr. Bernard Johns. "This is Jake Barnes, the man who's doing the investigation," she said to the group.

"So you're conducting some kind of inquiry into Angela's death?" asked a well-dressed man of about forty whose nametag said 'Bill.'

"That's right," Jake responded.

"What on heavens for?" Bill demanded. "She got sick and died. Case closed."

"It's never that simple," Jake said. "I was just hired this week. I can't tell you any more than that."

"What are your qualifications, if I may ask?" a member of the group named Elliott demanded.

"Thirty years as a member of the Albany Police Department, for starters," Jake answered. "In fact, I was the investigator on a case involving a member of your little circle here." He looked at Bernard Johns whose face lost all color.

"What do you mean?" Bill demanded. "Something to do with Bernie? What'd you do, Bernie, loose a tooth?" That brought laughter from everyone in the group, including Johns.

"Something like that," the dentist managed to say.

"You're not saying that you think one of us had anything to do with her death, are you, Barnes?" Elliott asked.

"As I said, I've just started, but I hope that you'll be willing to cooperate. I'd like to ask a few questions of everyone who was on the trip."

There were murmurs from several people, but no direct responses at first.

"Of course we will," Elliott said. "We've nothing to hide. It was a tragic accident, but that's all it was."

"Time will tell," Jake said. "Nice meeting you all." He turned and headed toward the exit. That turned out better than I could have expected, he told himself. If he did contribute to Boyer's death, Johns will start sweating. *Good. Let him sweat.*

Peter G. Pollak

10

Tuesday, June 15: 9:30 a.m.

One thing Jake discovered during the first weeks of his investigation was that detective work went a lot slower when you didn't have the power of the badge behind you. It took days to put together a number of interviews with people from the Mexico trip. To start, he had to run down the names and contact information for the people who had participated. He had trouble getting through to some people and not everyone of those he did reach, was willing to talk.

The person Jake was most anxious to talk to was Karen Crosetti, the woman who had been identified in the newspaper as Angela Boyer's roommate at the lodge in Oaxaca. Crosetti, however, refused to meet with him or answer questions on the phone.

Jake guessed that she had been told by a lawyer not to discuss the matter with anyone. Some people might argue that she bore some responsibility for the fact that Angela Boyer did not get prompt medical treatment. He could understand that she would want to avoid helping someone make that case, but her unwillingness to talk made his job that much harder. He didn't want to take no for an answer, but decided to work on the rest of the list and then come back to Crosetti later on.

The second person Jake pursued for an interview was Charlotte Richards, the singles club's representative on the trip. Richards, a realtor, agreed to meet at her office.

Richards accepted Jake's opening statement that the family wanted an independent investigation into Angela's death. That made his job a lot easier.

"When did you become aware that Ms. Boyer was sick?" Jake began.

Richards thought for a moment. "It had to be when we got back from our day trip to the ruins at *Lambityeco*. She was not on that trip. I thought she must have gone with Dr. Johns' group into the city. They told me they were going to do some shopping at the market."

"What made you think she'd gone with them?"

"She seemed to hang out with Dr. Johns and his friends. I just assumed she was with them."

"How did you learn that she was more than a little indisposed?"

"I ran into Marlene Fitzpatrick in the hall when I got back from our day trip. She was on her way to find Dr. Smythe. She told me Angela was very sick. I asked her to keep me informed. About a half an hour later, when I hadn't heard from her, I thought I'd better investigate, so I went to Angela's room. Dr. Smythe was there. He informed me that the hotel had sent for an ambulance."

"That must have been upsetting."

"It was. I was shocked and very concerned."

"Who else was in the room?"

"Marlene and Karen, who was Angela's roommate."

"Did you ask them any questions?"

"I did. I asked when Angela had taken ill. Marlene said she hadn't come to dinner the night before. Karen said she wasn't sure."

"Wasn't Karen's answer surprising?"

"In what way?" Richards asked.

"She was Angela's roommate, wasn't she?"

"True, but I don't think they were bosom buddies."

"But aren't roommates supposed to keep an eye on each other on trips like this?"

"We're not the Girl Scouts, but I suppose it was strange that she didn't mention it to me or the hotel management."

"Perhaps she did—mention it to the hotel, I mean."

"That's possible, in which case they have some explaining to do, don't they?"

"Miss Crosetti is not willing to talk to me," Jake admitted. "Can you think of any reason why she wouldn't?"

Richards shook her head.

"What happened next?" Jake asked.

"We waited for the ambulance. Dr. Smythe did all that he could to bring down her fever."

"Was Dr. Smythe on the trip in an official capacity as a medical officer?"

"No. He was there like everyone else . . . to see Mexico and have a good time. We used a reputable travel agency to plan the trip. I'm sure they consider medical, among other concerns for the well-being of the travelers on all their trips. In my opinion, this was just a tragic accident of fate."

"One last question," Jake said. "What kind of medical precautions does your club take in advance of a trip like this?"

"A lot," Richards said. "This was our first overseas trip. So we researched it carefully and gave everyone who was thinking of participating lots of information on health and safety issues."

"What kind of information?" Jake asked.

"We scheduled the trip far enough in advance so that those who wanted to attend would be able to get their passports and other documents in order. We sent out extensive information about health matters so that anyone who needed to take medications along would have time to get their prescriptions filled and we required people to fill out forms indicating any health issues we needed to be aware of, including what medications they would be bringing with them on the trip."

"So everyone had to fill out that form?"

"Absolutely. We allowed no exceptions."

"I'd like to take a look at the one Angela filled out and perhaps a few others."

"We couldn't allow you to see any of them without permission of the party involved. In Angela's case, however, I think we can assume her family would permit it, given that you are investigating her death on their behalf. I'll find out where the records are being stored and let you know when and where you can see them."

"Thank you."

"By the way, the materials we sent out warned people about drinking local water in places that might have lower standards of purity. I'm just guessing, but I suspect that's how Angela came in contact with the meningitis bacteria."

"You think she drank some bad water?" Jake asked.

Richards shrugged her shoulders. "Of course, I don't know that for certain, but isn't that the most logical explanation?"

"That's what I'm trying to find out," Jake replied.

The next day, Jake met with a bartender by the name of Marc Nicholson. Nicholson's name had appeared in one of the news stories about Boyer's death. He'd been quoted as saying that no one had any idea that Angela Boyer was ill. If he talked to a newspaper reporter, he'd probably talk to Jake.

Nicholson worked at the Green Door Tavern on upper Central Avenue. Jake dropped in mid-afternoon, hoping to find him present and with time on his hands. He was in luck on both counts.

Nicholson had little of value to add to the press accounts. He admitted that he'd spent most of his time wooing another woman on the trip and had not paid any attention to Boyer's comings and goings.

When questioned about the day of her death, Nicholson recalled that he was resting on his bed when he heard a commotion in the corridor outside his room. When he got up to find out what was going on, he learned that one of the members of the group had fallen ill and that an ambulance had been sent for from the nearest hospital.

"Did you notice whether Angela Boyer had spent most of her time with any particular individuals or group during the trip?" Jake asked.

"Sorry," Nicholson replied. "I can't even recall who she roomed with."

Nicholson did give Jake contact information for three members of the Mexico trip with a promise that he'd call Jake if he thought of anything that might explain why no one noticed that Boyer was so ill until it was too late.

Jake spent the following day trying to reach the people whose contact information he'd obtained from Nicholson.

The first person he reached was Stacey Winthrop—the woman Marc Nicholson said he'd spent most of his time with on the trip. Winthrop was an elementary school teacher who told Jake on the phone that she had not known Boyer prior to the trip. She supported Nicholson's story that the two of them hung around with a younger group of people and didn't interact much with Boyer and her friends. Jake didn't see any need to interview her in person.

The next name from Nicholson's list was Marlene Fitzpatrick—one of the women he'd met at the singles club event. It turned out that Marlene was a physical therapist—like Angela Boyer—and had treated Nicholson after a skiing accident, which is how he got to know her. She agreed to meet Jake and suggested a location: a diner on Wolf Road near her medical offices.

Jake arrived early in order to find a table that offered some privacy. Ms. Fitzpatrick arrived on time. She was an attractive woman of average height with short dirty-blond hair who looked to be in her mid-to-late thirties.

Jake greeted her and thanked her for agreeing to talk to him. While they waited for the waitress to bring Fitzpatrick a diet soda, Jake stated, in broad terms, the reason for the investigation. "The Boyer family wants to make sure that nothing important about Angela's death has been overlooked."

"Does that mean they are looking to cast blame?" she asked.

"Only if there is just cause," he replied. "They do have some questions they'd like me to ask all of the people on the trip. Is that okay?"

She hesitated, but eventually agreed when Jake pressed her.

"Tell me what you recall of Boyer before she got sick," he asked. "Did she spend her time with any particular individual or group of people?"

"She was one of a group of six or seven of us who did things together," she said. "There was Angela, Elliott Jorgensen, Bill Parsons, Ellen Bartlett, Beverly Harris, and myself. Oh, and the dentist, Bernard Johns."

"Angela's roommate wasn't in that group?" Jake asked.

"No, she hung out with a different crowd. Even though they were rooming together, she and Angela were not friends."

"Since you knew Angela, may I ask why weren't you rooming with her?"

"I had mentioned it to her at the meeting before the trip, but she had already agreed to room with her best friend—Roxanne Miner. Then Roxanne's mother was in a car accident and she had to cancel. By then, I'd already agreed to room with Ellen Bartlett."

"Did Angela pair off with any of the guys in a romantic way?" Jake asked.

"I believe that she had been dating Dr. Johns for a while, but she seemed to want to keep things cool during this trip."

"How do you mean? Did she say anything directly to you about Johns?"

"Not to me, but I noticed that she was having a conversation with him on the day we arrived and seemed upset. So I asked her if anything was wrong."

"What did she say?"

"She said 'Someone is having a hard time taking "no" for an answer.'"

"Those were her exact words?" Jake asked.

She nodded.

"Did anyone else hear her say that?"

"Ellen Bartlett might have. She was sitting right there. The two of us had been going over some brochures."

After a few more general questions, Jake turned to the subject of Boyer's illness.

"When did you become aware that Angela wasn't feeling well?" Jake asked.

She looked away. She was obviously uncomfortable talking about the subject. "I have thought about that a lot because I keep wondering how I didn't notice that she was so ill."

"Please explain."

"It was the night before she died," she continued. "Toward the end of dinner, I noticed that she wasn't in the dining room. I asked a couple of people at our table. Dr. Johns said he'd spoken to her and she was feeling indisposed."

"Are you certain it was Bernard Johns?"

"Positive. But he made it seem like she had a headache or something minor. So I didn't think about it any further until the next day." Marlene had to get out a tissue out of her purse to dab her eyes. "Sorry."

"I understand," Jake replied.

"Where was I?"

"The next morning."

"Oh, yes," she said. "I noticed Angela wasn't at breakfast and so I looked for Dr. Johns to see if he knew anything further, but he wasn't there. When I asked if anyone had seen him, someone said he'd gotten up early to take the van into the city with a few other people."

She had to stop and dab her eyes again.

"Did you talk to anyone else at that time about Angela––her roommate, Karen Crosetti, for example?"

"I did. I found her with her friends and I asked her about Angela. She said she was still asleep when she went into the room to get some things for that day's excursion."

"Was she aware that Ms. Boyer hadn't been feeling well?"

"It didn't seem like it. I got the impression that she'd been spending her nights in her boyfriend's room and wasn't paying any attention to what Angela was doing."

"Then what did you do?"

"It was getting close to the time we needed to line up for the bus. I had to go back to my room to freshen up and get my camera, but on the way, I went to Angela's room and knocked on the door. There was no answer. I tried the door, but it was locked. So, I just . . ."

Marlene couldn't hold back the tears. She had to rummage through her purse to find additional tissues. When she got herself under control, she finished her sentence. "I didn't say anything to anyone. I just went on that damn excursion and worried about her all day. I'm still so angry with myself for not having stayed back to try to find out if she was all right."

"You shouldn't blame yourself," Jake said. "You didn't know the illness was life-threatening."

"But I should have made more of an effort to find out. We all should have. We just let her die."

Jake waited several minutes to let her compose herself. "I only have a few more questions," he said.

She nodded.

"When you got back from the field trip, did you notice if Dr. Johns or any of the people who had gone with him into the city were back?"

"Let me think. No, I don't recall."

"Okay. Then what happened?"

"When I got back, I went to Angela's room and found the door still locked. So I went looking for Angela's roommate. She was on the patio having a drink. I told her someone needed to check to see if Angela was in her room."

She waited for Jake, who was taking notes, to catch up. "Karen and I went to the room and she opened the door. The room was dark and smelled bad. Angela was in her bed lying on her face with a trash basket on the floor next to the bed. I could see that she was very sick. I told Karen I was going to get Dr. Smythe. He had been on the excursion and was in his room. I told him it was an emergency. He came back to Angela's room with me."

She stopped to blow her nose. "I'm sorry," she said. "This is so difficult."

Jake nodded. "Take your time," he said.

Marlene nodded. "I was in the room when he examined Angela," she said. "It didn't take him long to see that she had a very high fever. He instructed us to try to cool her down by putting her in the bathtub and giving her a cool sponge bath while he talked to the people at the front desk."

"We literally had to carry Angela into the bathroom. She couldn't stand on her own and was totally incoherent. We put her in the tub and started running the water. I had to hold her up to prevent her from sliding under the water. She was that weak."

She waited again while Jake took notes. "Finally, Dr. Smythe returned. He said that the lodge had called the hospital and that they were sending an ambulance. Later, he told me he wanted the lodge to drive her to the hospital, but they refused, saying the hospital had told them to keep her there."

Jake nodded. "How long did it take for the ambulance to arrive?"

"It seemed like hours. I was beside myself with worry."

"Did Dr. Smythe administer any medications to Angela during that time?"

"I'm not sure. We tried to get her temperature down in the bath and I know he tried to get her to drink some fruit juice."

"How did she seem?" Jake asked.

"Terrible. Weak and incoherent."

"Did Dr. Smythe go with her to the hospital?"

"Yes. I wanted to go also, but they wouldn't let me. That was the worst night of my life. I finally got a couple hours of sleep before someone knocked on my door. It was the hotel staff to let us know that we were wanted in the conference room. That's when they announced that she hadn't made it."

Jake let her take some time to compose herself. "Marlene, I know you feel you should have done more, but you did everything anyone could have expected of you or anyone else. It was illogical that she would have contracted bacterial meningitis. That's why I'm conducting this investigation."

"What do you think happened?"

"It's too early to say, but I hope to know more after talking to the rest of the people on the trip."

It was early in his investigation, but after speaking with Marlene Fitzpatrick, Jake was convinced more than ever that his suspicions about Angela Boyer's death were justified. Dr. Johns had to have known that she had more than a headache and he did nothing about it. The logic of that understanding, however, was a long way from having proof that would hold up in a court of law.

11

Friday, June 18: 12:30 p.m.

Friday just after noon, Jake was at a table in Spinelli's waiting for Chloe Boyer. Before he left home, he'd tried to think of some tasks to keep her off his back while he continued to interview people from the Mexican singles trip. Chloe, as usual, was late. This time she apologized.

"I was at Crossgates," she said, referring to the large shopping center by way of explanation.

"Not a problem," Jake answered, although he was beginning to question his decision to let her work on the case with him. Of course, he couldn't fire her, since that would cut off his funding source and put an end to his investigation. Plus, she wasn't interfering with his work . . . yet.

"So, have you found out anything?" Chloe asked after she ordered her usual salad and diet Coke.

"Nothing conclusive. I met with Elliott Jorgensen and Beverly Harris yesterday. Neither added anything that I didn't already know. Bill Parsons has been giving me the runaround, telling me that he's too busy and that he doesn't know anything. I had to press him hard, making it seem as if he could save himself from being called as a witness if it comes to a trial before he agreed to meet with me. I'm meeting him at 5 o'clock today."

"Can I come?"

"I don't think that would be a good idea," Jake replied.

"Why not?" she demanded.

"Because he might be reluctant to say certain things with the victim's sister sitting at the table."

She shrugged. "I guess so. What does Parsons do?"

"He's a broker in the Albany's Merrill Lynch office."

"Oh, one of those."

Jake just had to ask. "One of those what?"

"You know," Chloe answered. "The kind that wants you to trust them with all of your money."

"I wouldn't know," Jake replied.

"So, what's next? When are you going to interview Dr. Johns?"

"There are several reasons we're not going to approach Johns yet. I want him to worry about what we're up to. Maybe he'll make a mistake of some kind."

"Like what?"

"Like trying to influence one of the other people on the trip not to talk to me or to create a certain picture of what went on."

"Okay.

"And, when I do approach him, I don't want to be on a fishing expedition. I want to be prepared to ask him some hard questions based on what I've learned about the events to see if he lies or contradicts what someone else has told me."

Chloe nodded. "That's smart."

"Standard operating procedure."

"So, when do we go to Mexico? You said you wanted to talk to the police there."

"I," Jake said, emphasizing the word, "will go to Mexico only if and when I am certain I know what to look for. That's why I need to talk to everyone who can shed any light on Angela's whereabouts during the days prior to her becoming ill."

"You're not taking me?"

"Chloe, I'm not sure if we need to go, but if I do go, I don't want to be worried about you instead of doing my job."

"I'm not fragile," Chloe replied, her face flushed, "And I'll bet my Spanish is better than yours."

"It probably is," Jake admitted.

"I think my grandmother would want me to go," she said after a minute, her face in a pout.

"Okay, Chloe," Jake replied. "I'll keep it in mind, but I'm not ready to go. I am just about ready to contact Dr. Smythe. I'm not certain that he'll speak to me, but if he's willing, I want to be able to ask the right questions— questions that can help us narrow down when and how Angela might have become infected."

"What can I do to help?" Chloe asked. "Say, I've got an idea," she said before Jake had a chance to answer. "Why don't I follow Bernard Johns? See who he's going out with in case someone else turns up, you know, missing?"

"No," Jake replied. "Out of the question. He'd spot you a mile away, get a lawyer, and take out a restraining order. That would be a disaster."

She appeared to be crushed. "I'm only trying to help."

"I understand, and you are helping," Jake said. "You're keeping your eyes and ears open for any information that might help, right?"

She nodded.

"Good then. I should be done with the interviews in a week's time."

"Oh, I almost forgot," Chloe said, rifling through her purse. "Here's some of the mail that was addressed to Angela . . . except for the bills. My dad took those."

She handed over about a half a dozen letters. Jake had asked her to monitor Angela's mail. There was always an off chance that something would show up that was interesting.

"Very good," Jake said as he scanned through the envelopes. There was one from a credit card company soliciting Angela as a client, there were a couple of advertisements from companies servicing the physical therapy community, and there was one from the Albany Singles Club. He opened that one. It contained a schedule of the club's upcoming events and meetings.

"I wonder," he said, looking through the meeting schedule.

"What?"

"You're single, right?"

She nodded.

"That means you can join the club."

"Become a member?"

"Why not? Let's see if Johns goes to the meetings. If so, you can observe him without invading his privacy."

"Okay," Chloe said. "Since you put it that way, I'm game."

"I want to know if he's dating anyone from the club . . . in particular, anyone from the Mexican trip group. Hang out with people your own age," Jake instructed, "but if you recognize any of Angela's friends, it's okay to talk to them. Keep the conversation casual. Don't say anything about the investigation or that you have any suspicions about Angela's death."

"What if Dr. Johns approaches me?" Chloe asked. "I did meet him a few times and he'd probably recognize me."

"That's where you'll have to call on your acting skills," Jake replied. "Don't ask him any personal questions. If he volunteers information, that's fine, but don't seem like you're interested in him. He probably got the impression that you didn't like him and would be suspicious if all of a sudden you acted the least bit interested."

12

Same Day: 5:15 p.m.

Singles club member and Merrill Lynch broker William Gregory Parsons insisted that Jake meet him after four in the afternoon in his office in downtown Albany. Because he was unable to find on-street parking, Jake was fortunate that there was underground parking for the building where Merrill Lynch had its offices. Another receipt to be added to his growing pile of expenses.

Parsons made him wait more than a half an hour. While sitting on a modern, but not very comfortable couch in the waiting room, Jake tried to make sense of the data scrolling across the large-screen TV behind the receptionist's desk. He recognized IBM and a couple of the other stock symbols, but the numbers were meaningless to him. He had a layman's suspicion of the stock market. A plaything for rich people was the kindest light he could shed on it.

Parsons came out with a bored look on his face. Jake estimated that he was in his early forties. His hair was thinning, but he dressed the role with a patterned red tie and highly polished shoes complementing his navy pinstriped trousers and blue shirt with white collar. Jake followed Parsons into a small conference room. A computer screen on the table displayed more obscure data, with numbers changing almost continuously. Jake had to turn away from it in order to concentrate on his subject.

"Let's make this quick, Barnes," Parsons said when both were seated. "It's been a busy day on the Street and I've still got some phone calls to make."

"I won't keep you any longer than necessary," Jake replied, although he felt like punching the guy in the jaw. "I have just a few questions. First, did you know Angela Boyer prior to the Mexico trip?"

"I had met her a few times, but look here, Barnes, on what authority are you asking these questions? You're retired from the police department, correct?"

"As I stated when we met at the singles club, I was hired by a member of Angela Boyer's family to conduct an investigation into the circumstances surrounding her unfortunate demise," Jake replied.

"Which member? I doubt that it was her father."

"I'm not at liberty to say, but we've been through all of this on the phone, Mr. Parsons. Would you like to see a copy of my detective's license? I have it here in my briefcase."

"Sure," Parsons replied.

Jake opened his briefcase and produced the document sent to him by the State of New York authorizing him to conduct business as a private investigator.

After Parsons studied the document and handed it back, Jake returned it to his briefcase and laid a yellow pad and two pens on the table. "Shall we get on with the questions so that you can make your phone calls?"

Parsons shrugged.

"So, you knew Angela Boyer. How well did you know her?"

"I'd met her at singles club meetings and we'd been on one or two trips prior to the Mexico trip."

"Did you ever date her?"

"No. A few of us went out together as a group a few times, but never one-on-one."

"Did you ever ask her out?"

"I didn't get the feeling that she was interested. So the answer is no."

"Did that bother you—that she didn't seem interested?"

Parsons frowned. "Not really. She was not the only attractive single woman living in Albany."

"How would you describe Angela Boyer?" Jake asked.

"Dead," Parsons said.

Jake looked up. This guy didn't have to try so hard to be annoying. "When she was alive," he said.

"Like I said," Parsons replied, "I didn't know her that well."

"From what you observed."

"Nice. Attractive. Outgoing."

"A lot of guys must have found her appealing. Did it ever strike you as odd that she was still single?"

Parsons sat back in his chair. "I guess I never gave it much thought. Women these days get into their careers."

"Any idea which it might have been?"

"Not really, but I thought this was going to be about Angela's death, not her life."

"I'm getting there, Mr. Parsons," Jake said, trying to keep his professional demeanor in the face of Parsons' desire to give him a hard time. "One last question and then we'll get to the trip. Were you aware of whom she was dating—over the past year, let's say?"

"What's the difference? She died of spinal meningitis. That's a disease, Barnes. She wasn't murdered."

"Are you a medical doctor, Mr. Parsons?" Jake demanded.

"Of course not."

"Then let's stick to those things you have direct knowledge of, shall we?"

Parsons sighed and looked up at the ceiling.

"Was she dating anyone from the club?"

Parsons turned back to face Jake. "You already know the answer."

"Bernard Johns?" Jake asked.

"Bingo."

"When did you become aware that Ms. Boyer was ill?"

"Not until the day she died," Parsons replied. "Some of us were planning a side trip that morning. Bernie—Dr. Johns—informed us that Angela wasn't feeling well and was planning on remaining at the lodge. When we got back, I went to take a shower and get dressed for dinner. When I came down to the restaurant, everyone was talking about her being sick and that an ambulance had been sent for. The next morning, they woke us up to tell us that she was dead."

"Oh, before I forget," Jake said, "who besides you and Bernard Johns went on this side trip?"

"Just Elliott Jorgensen."

"It must have been pretty upsetting when you learned that Angela Boyer was dead," Jake stated.

"Of course. She went so fast. It was hard to believe that nothing could have been done."

"Were you concerned that whatever had killed her might be contagious?"

"I'll admit that was my first thought, but I was not the only one. If the rest of us were in danger, we needed to know."

"Meningitis can be contagious. Did they tell you that?"

"Not at first. I was pretty pissed about it for a while, but when they explained that you had to have direct contact, I calmed down."

"Who was in charge at that point?"

"That was one of the problems. Charlotte Richards was the trip coordinator, but she didn't have any information. It had the makings of an effing disaster for a while there."

Jake nodded.

"Finally, Richards brought us together and told us that a doctor was coming from the city to the lodge and that he would be bringing a supply of antibiotics in case anyone else had symptoms. The group was pretty much on edge the whole day. We voted to terminate the trip and were also waiting to hear about arrangements to get back home. Fortunately, no one else experienced symptoms and we all got back here safely."

"How did Dr. Johns seem through all of this?"

"I don't know . . . like the rest of us, I suppose—upset, concerned. Why do you ask?"

"He'd been dating her."

"I don't know how serious they were."

"Even so, you'd think he'd have more interest in her welfare than most other people on the trip."

"I suppose so. What are you driving at?"

"I'm not driving at anything other than asking you how he appeared to you while all this was happening. Did he seem especially concerned when he came back from having asked Ms. Boyer to join you?"

"No, not that I can remember. I didn't get the impression that she was seriously ill—just under the weather."

"What about when you got back from your day trip? Do you remember if Dr. Johns said anything about checking up on her?"

Parsons thought a minute. "I don't recall if he did or didn't."

"Doesn't that seem odd to you?"

"That I can't recall? No, it seems as if I can't recall."

"I'm not questioning your memory," Jake said. "I'm saying if a woman you'd been dating had not been feeling well, wouldn't you check in on her first thing after you'd been gone for a while?"

"Possibly, but who says he didn't?"

"No one. I'm just trying to find out if he expressed concern or stated that he was planning to check on her."

"Again, all I can say is I don't recall."

"But if he did seem anxious about checking in on her and said something about it, wouldn't you have remembered?"

"I don't know whether I would or wouldn't. We had been out in the sun all day. I was just thinking about taking a nice long shower. That's the best I can tell you, Barnes. If you want to hang something on Bernie Johns, I'm not going to help you do it. There's nothing to hang on him."

"I'm not trying to hang anything on anyone," Jake said. "I'm trying to understand just what happened and why no one noticed that Ms. Boyer had become fatally ill until it was too late to save her life."

Parsons looked at his watch. "I can't help you there. Look, I've answered your questions. Now I really have to end this. I have work to do before I call it a day."

Parsons accepted Jake's handshake and escorted him to the reception area.

Jake sat for a few minutes in his car before starting it up. Maybe Parsons had helped him more than he knew. If the other people on the trip corroborated Parsons' testimony that Johns had not seemed anxious to check up on Angela Boyer, that would suggest that he didn't want anyone to learn about her condition, and that suggested that he was responsible for her being in that condition in the first place. It was a long shot, he knew, but until the facts proved otherwise, that was a theory he planned on pursuing.

Peter G. Pollak

13

Wednesday, June 23: 7:00 p.m.

Jake was surprised when Dr. Randolph Smythe, the doctor who had been on the Mexico trip, agreed to meet him. Smythe did not have to do so and he had a lot to lose if the investigation revealed that he contributed to Angela Boyer's death either by something he did or something he should have done. On the other hand, if he refused to meet with Jake, he would be casting suspicion on himself. When he arrived for the interview, Smythe insisted that his lawyer sit in. Jake had no choice but to accept those terms. He was not was not out to get Dr. Smythe and wanted him to be cooperative.

Jake was not familiar with the lawyer, whose name was Fred Nathanson. He was a short, thin man whose suit looked like it was a size too large. His business card indicated that his office was in the same building where Dr. Smythe maintained his offices, which suggested Smythe had retained him at the last minute. The lawyer laid out the terms of the interview. Jake would ask his questions and would give the lawyer a chance to advise his client before he answered any of them.

Dr. Smythe was a forty-one-year-old divorced dermatologist. It appeared that his practice was modest, judging by the age of the building in which he maintained an office, the small size of the waiting room, and Dr. Smythe's personal office, which was only large enough for a desk, chairs for two visitors and a filing cabinet.

Dr. Smythe had chosen to meet at seven in the evening, presumably so as not to interfere with seeing his patients. He was a pleasant enough man; his handshake was warm and his smile genuine. He was a few inches taller than Jake, was beginning to go bald, and wore wire-rimmed glasses.

"Let me clear one thing up right away," he said while Jake was removing his yellow pad from his briefcase.

"What's that?"

"I was not on that trip in any official medical capacity."

"I am aware of that," Jake said.

"Even though we were traveling out of the country, it was not as if we were going to India or someplace where you might want to have a doctor as part of your group. I am a member of the club because I'm single. I went on the trip to have a good time."

"Unfortunately, that was not what happened."

"No, you're quite right about that. I found myself in the midst of a crisis that had a tragic ending."

Jake thought for a moment. "What about the resort where you were staying?"

"How so?"

"In terms of medical staff and arrangements. They must deal with people getting sick or injured all the time."

"I believe so," Smythe said. "They told us that their staff is trained to handle emergencies. Plus, the hospital is only an hour away. In ninety-nine out of one hundred cases, that's probably sufficient."

"When did you become aware that Ms. Boyer was sick?"

Dr. Smythe looked at the lawyer, who nodded. "I believe it was the fifth afternoon after our arrival. A woman came to my room, said a member of the group was ill, and asked if I could take a look." Dr. Smythe took a sip of water from a plastic water bottle. "At that point I had no idea how serious a matter it was. The woman—Marlene Fitzpatrick her name is—said Ms. Boyer had been sick in bed all day. I was thinking dysentery or perhaps food poisoning. That it could be meningitis never crossed my mind."

"Why do you think Ms. Fitzpatrick came to you rather than go to the hotel staff?"

"Good question. I'm not sure. You'll have to ask her."

"What did you see when you got to Ms. Boyer's room?"

"There was evidence that she had been throwing up. Her roommate was trying to get her to drink some water. I did a quick exam—although I didn't have any medical instruments with me. I could see that she was burning up and was probably dehydrated. She was unable to answer my questions and appeared to be in great discomfort. I asked the roommate how long she'd been sick and she said she didn't know for sure, but at least a day."

"Those were her exact words?"

"Yes, I believe so."

"Could you try to reconstruct that conversation—what you asked her and what she replied?"

Dr. Smythe thought for a minute. "I believe I said 'How long has she been this way?' The roommate replied, 'I can't say for certain, but at least since sometime yesterday.'"

"Okay, thank you," Jake said. "Continue."

"I told Marlene and the roommate—whose name, I think, was Karen—to get her into the bathroom and give her a lukewarm bath to cool her down. I went down to the front desk and said we had a medical emergency and needed to get a member of our group to the hospital. The person at the desk was very calm. She asked me some questions and then said she would call the hospital right away. I waited while she called. My Spanish is not good enough for me to have been able to follow everything that was said. When the clerk hung up, she said that they would send an ambulance right away. I asked wouldn't it be faster if we brought her to the hospital, but the clerk said the hospital told her to wait for the ambulance."

"Then what happened?"

"I told the clerk to bring them into Angela's room and went back to assist the women. They had carried Ms. Boyer into the bathroom and were trying to cool her off with cold washcloths. At that point, she was unable to stand up on her own and was delirious. Eventually, we brought her back to her bed and waited."

"How long did it take for the ambulance to get there?"

"Approximately an hour."

"What did they do when they got there?"

"They could see that she was severely dehydrated. So they ran an IV. I suggested that they begin an antibiotic cocktail, but I don't know if they did so."

"Did you know it was meningitis at that point?"

"No. I didn't find out until the next day. That's when we were told the cause of her death. A number of possibilities were going through my mind, but all I knew was she needed to be taken to a hospital as fast as possible."

"Do you think the ambulance crew recognized the symptoms?"

"I couldn't understand what they were saying to each other and didn't know how well they understood me. They kept saying '*Si, señor*' when I made suggestions, but whether they were doing what I suggested or understood me, I don't know."

"But you went with the ambulance, correct?"

"I did. That was a ride I'll never forget. She was starting to convulse. There was a lot of conversation between the attendants. At one point, the driver called ahead on his phone. The hospital was prepared for her when we arrived. I just think we had discovered her too late to save her life."

"Why do you think that is?"

"I don't have a clue. I suppose her roommate might be questioned about that. Have you spoken to her?"

"She's on my list," Jake replied. "Anyone else?"

"It's hard to say. What about the trip leader, Charlotte Richards? She should have known that Angela had not signed up for any of that day's events."

"I have spoken with Ms. Richards," Jake said. "She says people were not required to partake of any of the daily trips or activities. Some people went off on their own; others stayed at the resort. She also claims she didn't know Angela was ill until that afternoon."

"It just seems that everything went wrong that could have gone wrong," Smythe mumbled.

Jake put his pad down. "What about the people she hung out with? Don't people tend to form small groups on these kinds of trips? Did you notice who her friends were on the trip?"

"Interesting question. Let me think for a minute."

Nathanson leaned over and whispered in Smythe's ear. "I know," he said to the lawyer.

"Although we'd only been there a few days, she was part of a group that ate together and seemed to do things together."

"Can you tell me who was in that group?"

"Marlene Fitzpatrick was, and Ellen Bartlett, and a few guys—Elliott Jorgensen, Bill Parsons, and, oh, of course, Bernie—Bernie Johns, the dentist."

"Why do you say 'of course'?"

"I believe he and Angela were dating, or at least I got that impression at a couple of club meetings that I'd attended."

"So shouldn't Dr. Johns, in particular, have been aware of Angela's being more than a little under the weather?"

"Possibly," Dr. Smythe replied. "Possibly not."

"How so?"

"Even trained medical professionals have a problem correctly diagnosing meningitis."

"I'm not talking about making an accurate diagnosis, Doctor," Jake replied. "What I'm wondering is how a friend, especially one who might have had a personal relationship with the deceased, could not have known that she needed medical attention?"

"That's a question you'll have to ask him," Mr. Nathanson said.

Jake nodded. "What I'm asking Dr. Smythe is, in your opinion, if they were her friends, whether they could have misunderstood or downplayed or ignored the fact that Ms. Boyer was too sick to even ask for help?"

"Anything's possible, Mr. Barnes," Smythe answered, "but I think you're asking a legitimate question. I'm just not the person who can provide an answer."

"Last question," Jake said. "Do you feel the club took the necessary precautions in advance of the trip, such as providing adequate warning about the dangers?"

"I do," Dr. Smythe replied. "You can't make people read the material that is sent to them or listen when the club leaders go over the information, but they did provide the information."

"I've learned that Angela Boyer had diabetes and that would have made her more susceptible to the disease."

"That's possible," Dr. Smythe said. "I'm not an endocrinologist."

"Okay. Thank you for your time," Jake replied, ending the interview.

14

Friday, June 25: 11:00 a.m.

Ellen Bartlett was the next to the last person from the Mexican trip on Jake's interview list. She was a marketing executive for a group of doctors and agreed to meet him in her office the day after he'd met with Dr. Smythe. Bartlett was a short brunette in her mid-to-late thirties. Her relaxed, but professional demeanor gave the impression that she was quite competent at what she did.

"How have things been going?" she asked after escorting Jake to her office. The office was neat and comfortable, as Jake would have expected. On the wall was the kind of abstract art that professional offices hang that has no particular meaning. He sat down in a green leatherette chair in front of her desk while she sat in her large black leatherette desk chair. "Have you learned anything earth-shattering or was I correct?"

"That there's nothing to learn?"

She nodded.

"There's always something to be learned, Ms. Bartlett."

"Please, call me, Ellen."

Jake smiled. "Ok, Ellen. There's always something to be learned."

"You know what I'm asking," Bartlett continued. "Have you found anything significant?"

"It's too early to draw any conclusions. We'll see what it adds up to when I've completed the process."

"So, what can I tell you?"

"Let's start by how well you knew Angela Boyer."

"We went to the same private school, actually. Miss Potter's. I'm sure you've heard of it. I was a year behind Angela. We weren't close friends, but we knew each other."

"Describe her as a person. Was she adventuresome or cautious?"

"Somewhere in the middle, I'd say."

"Outgoing or shy?"

"More on the outgoing side, but not overly so."

"A leader or a follower?"

"She was more of a follower, but if she had an opinion, she'd express it."

"I understand that she was dating Dr. Johns at the time of this trip."

"I believe so."

"And, on the trip, did they seem like a couple? Did they hold hands, sit together at meals . . . that kind of thing?"

"No, they didn't. I got the sense that she either wanted to keep things cool during the trip or perhaps end the relationship all together."

"Did that seem to bother Dr. Johns?"

"If it did, he didn't let on. However, he was quieter than usual for the first few days of the trip. He told me that he was just getting over a case of the flu."

"Really?"

"I noticed that he looked pale when we got off the plane. I thought it might have been the effects of the flight, but then he wasn't himself the next day either."

"When you say he wasn't his usual self, can you be more specific?"

"Usually he's in the middle of every conversation. Sometimes I think he tries too hard, but not so at the beginning of the trip."

"Did you ask him about it?"

"Yes. We were getting off our bus at the end of the first day and I noticed that he still seemed wobbly. So I said something to him. He told me that he was getting over the flu. It wasn't until the day before Angela got sick that he was back to his old self."

"Interesting," Jake replied. "So, when did you learn that Angela was sick?"

"Hmm. Let me think. We were going on a trip to one of the archaeological sites. Marlie went to see if Angela was coming with us or going into town with the guys."

"By Marlie you mean Marlene Fitzpatrick?"

"Yes, sorry. She calls me Ellie, so I call her Marlie."

"Okay, go on."

"When Marlie came back alone, she said the door to Angela's room was locked."

"What happened when you got back from the trip? Can you recall how it was discovered that she was seriously ill?"

"When we got off the bus, Marlie said she was going to look in on Angela. I was tired. So I told her I was going back to the room to rest before dinner. I fell asleep; when I woke up, Marlie wasn't there, so I went to look for her. That's when I learned that she was with Angela and they'd sent for the ambulance."

"What about Dr. Johns? Did you see him during that time?"

"Yes. Everyone had gathered in the lounge area. He was sitting with Bill Parsons, Elliott Jorgensen, and a few others."

"Did you talk to them?"

She nodded.

"What did you say?"

"'Did you hear about Angela?' or something like that."

"How did they respond?"

"Everyone nodded. ' Awful, isn't it?' Dr. Johns said. 'How bad is she?' I asked. Bill said they didn't know. Just that an ambulance had been sent for."

"Dr. Johns used the word 'awful'?"

Ellen nodded.

"Then what?" Jake asked.

"I went to get a drink, then joined them. They were talking about the market in town. I guess people were asking about it."

"Was there any further discussion about Angela?"

"Not until the ambulance came. Then we all got up and waited in the lobby. They finally wheeled her out. Marlie was in tears. She wanted to go with them, but they only had room for Dr. Smythe."

"Then what?"

"Eventually we all went to the dining room and had dinner."

"How did Dr. Johns seem? Was he very upset?"

"He seemed to think that she'd be okay. He kept telling people not to worry, that the Mexican medical system was competent and up-to-date."

"Interesting," Jake said. "So he wasn't worried?"

She shook her head. "He didn't appear to be."

After Jake finished his interview with Ellen Bartlett, he went back to his house and added the information she had provided to his timeline document. Discovering that Bernard Johns had been sick at the start of the Mexico trip might prove to be significant. He was getting better just as Angela Boyer came down with meningitis. Could there be a connection?

Jake realized he needed to talk to a specialist. It took a couple days around an intervening weekend, but he managed to get an appointment with Professor Leon Clarke of the Albany Medical School.

It was a long walk from the visitor's parking garage to the building where Professor Clarke had his office. Jake was sweating by the time he arrived and thankful for the building's air conditioning. Professor Clarke was a squat, balding man with a pleasant smile in his late thirties or early forties. Clarke retreated behind his desk after walking Jake from the reception area to his cubbyhole of an office.

"Thank you very much for agreeing to meet with me, Professor Clarke."

"How can I help you?"

"As I explained over the phone," Jake replied, "I'm investigating the possible murder of a thirty-four-year-old woman. What it comes down to is the following question: Would it be possible for someone to intentionally infect another person with bacterial meningitis?"

"Wow. Tough question. Theoretically, yes, but . . . practically, it would be exceedingly difficult. Can you tell me more details?"

"Certainly," Jake said. "The person whom I suspect committed the murder was reported to be 'under the weather' at the start of a singles group trip to Mexico. The suspect explained his lack of energy by telling a friend that he had been sick with the flu. A few days later, the woman that he had been dating came down with what later turned out to be meningitis. She died, in part, because her illness was not discovered in time. I believe the suspect knew she was seriously ill and failed to report it or get help. That's why I'm wondering if he had something to do with her becoming infected."

"I see. Did you know that contracting meningitis in Mexico, unfortunately, happens to a number of people annually?"

"So I've read," Jake replied. "But that fact may only have added cover for the murder."

Prof. Clarke thought about that for a moment. "So you think the man somehow carried the bacteria and transmitted it to the victim without suffering more than flu-like symptoms himself?"

Jake nodded. "That's what I'm trying to understand. Would that even be possible, and, if so, how might someone do that?"

"Again, all I can say without having any hard data in my hands is that that would be extremely risky to the perpetrator without guaranteeing success."

"Okay. Would the fact that the woman was a diabetic help? I am correct, am I not, in saying that diabetics who contact the bacteria are more likely to experience severe symptoms?"

"For the most part, that is correct."

"I'd say that was the beauty of his plan. Whether she lived or not, it was extremely unlikely that her illness would be traced to him."

Dr. Clarke nodded. "Unless someone did blood work on both of them at the time, that's true."

"Would it change your mind if you knew that the perpetrator was a medical professional?"

"That certainly would increase the chances that someone could pull off such a plan, but there is still a major problem you're overlooking."

"What's that?" Jake asked.

"How did he obtain the bacteria in the first place? Unless he works in a lab where he could obtain the bacteria, you can't just order it from your corner drug store."

"I had thought of that and I don't have the answer . . . yet. Just for your information, the suspect is a dentist."

"Which reduces the likelihood that he had access to the bacteria and that he knew how to handle it, if he somehow was able to obtain it."

"If I could get a blood sample today—more than a month after the fact—would there be any signs that he had been exposed to the bacteria?"

"Possibly," Dr. Clarke replied, "but that would take a court order, right?"

Jake nodded.

As he drove back to his house, Jake felt overwhelmed by the difficulty of trying to prove Johns' complicity in Angela Boyer's death. Had someone investigated on the spot—maybe taken a sample of Dr. Johns' blood—then a case might have been established, but given the passage of time and Jake's lack of access to the crime scene, it seemed as if only a confession would convict Johns of having infected Angela Boyer.

That left one issue open—why hadn't he acted to get medical help for Boyer?

Even if he hadn't exposed Boyer to the meningitis bacteria, Dr. Johns had to have recognized how sick she was on the morning he left her alone. By not letting someone know about her condition, he contributed to her death. Had he intended to do so? Again, unless he confessed, was there any way of proving that he had?

15

Thursday, July 8: 3:45 p.m.

July 4th came and went. Jake tried unsuccessfully to keep his mind off Bernard Johns. While he was standing at the grill in his backyard cooking hot dogs and hamburgers for Mikey, Mary, and a few friends, he wondered if Dr. Johns was enjoying himself with some new woman who was innocent of the danger she might have placed herself in. While he watched Mikey and his friend, Elvis, running through the backyard sprinkler, he wondered if Dr. Johns was eyeing his next victim at an ocean beach or fancy swimming pool. And that night, instead of paying attention to the movie on the TV, he speculated on whether Dr. Johns was sitting at his desk plotting out another perfect crime.

Tuesday's mail brought some relief to his mental anguish. The State of New York would permit him to examine their file on Betsy Lunsford's death. The letter told him which office to call to arrange to see the materials. Jake immediately made the call, but to his dismay, he was told it would be a week before they could be made available. He agreed to be there the following Tuesday. When he hung up the phone, he took the dog for a walk, trying to come up with some constructive way to spend the week. He'd finished the last of the Mexico trip interviews the previous week, with one exception—Bernard Johns himself.

Jake wondered if Johns was concerned that he hadn't received a phone call. A criminal with an alibi wants to get that alibi into the record. Johns undoubtedly had a story well rehearsed concerning his lack of awareness of Angela's condition and was undoubtedly dying to tell it. Jake, on the other hand, didn't want to give him the satisfaction.

To keep himself from sneaking a doughnut when he got back from his walk, Jake got out the lawn mower and mowed a patch in the front of his house that grew faster than the rest of his lawn because of some fertilizer that he'd thrown on it a few weeks back. Then he swept the floor of his garage for a while. Spying his barely used golf clubs in the corner of the garage, he decided to spend the afternoon at a driving range on the edge of the city.

After paying $10 for a bucket of thirty well-used golf balls, Jake took out his frustrations hitting every ball in the bucket in rapid succession. Most of them screeched well left or right of his target, but he didn't care. After that, he sat on a bench and drank a diet soda, watching the other duffers. With nothing better to do, he hit a second bucket, taking only slightly more time than he did with the first.

The following Tuesday, Jake was out the door as soon as Mikey was safely on his way to his school. It took two hours to drive to the New Paltz State Police headquarters, where he was to be allowed to examine the folder on Betsy Lunsford's death.

Before the State Police allowed him to examine their records, he had to fill out various forms, swearing that he would neither alter any of the documents nor remove them permanently from the folder. Then, after being placed in a room with only a pad of paper and a handful of pencils to use to take notes, the Lunsford folder was handed over to him.

He spent a good two hours going through the few documents in the folder. As he suspected, there was no useful information concerning how she'd fallen. The person who wrote up the final report speculated that she'd fallen from a location between an hour and ninety minutes from the base, although the exact location could not be determined. The height of the fall virtually guaranteed her death, not to mention the fact that her body was not discovered for several days.

The only information in the folder that was new and potentially useful was the transcript of interviews conducted with various people who had hiked in the area the day that Lunsford went missing. While no one reported seeing or hearing her fall, several people did make note of her car in the parking lot. Lunsford drove a late model, white Audi S6. When asked if they noticed any of the other cars in the lot, only one person could remember another car by name and model. A SUNY New Paltz student stated that he remembered seeing a Mazda Miata in the lot when he arrived that Sunday morning to hike the Devil's Way Trail. He remembered it clearly because he was a big fan of the Miata. He recalled having spent a few minutes examining the car close up to learn the year and condition of the vehicle.

It turned out that the car was a rare 1990 hardtop. Mazda only started making the Miata the year before. The interviewer had asked the student whether the car was still there when he and his fellow hikers returned later that day. It was gone, he stated. He'd been disappointed because he hoped to talk to the owner. Unfortunately, the student couldn't remember what state issued the car's license plate.

None of the other people interviewed by the State Police had either remembered the Miata or claimed ownership of the car.

Tracing the owner of the Miata would not be easy, but, at the moment, Jake didn't have any other leads to pursue. The next day he stopped at the local Mazda dealership. They put him in touch with an official from Mazda USA, who stated quite firmly that they would not release any ownership records unless Jake obtained a court order. Another dead end!

After a fruitless trip, the next day, to the library to try to uncover the owner of the Miata in newspaper stories about the car, Jake sat in his truck in his driveway, thinking. He felt at a total and utter dead end. There was no other way of putting it. He'd finished interviewing all of the trip participants who would talk to him and, while the interview with Elliott Jorgensen confirmed that Bernard Johns had not said anything about checking in on Angela Boyer when they returned from their side trip, that, by itself, didn't prove that he was responsible for infecting her with the meningitis bacteria.

Adding to his feeling of frustration, the medical report on Angela's death added no useful information in terms of how Boyer had contracted the disease. Chloe had come through in obtaining the document and having it translated. The document, however, just contained the bare minimum information—name and age of victim, time of arrival at the hospital, and so forth.

Could either Dr. Smythe or the ambulance crew have done anything differently that would have saved Angela's life? While the Boyer family may have an interest in that question, it was not one that Jake wanted to pursue. He wasn't interested in hanging her death on either party. How they responded that April afternoon shed no light on how she'd become infected in the first place or why it took so long for someone to discover the extent of her illness.

Trying to find out whether other cases of meningitis were reported from the same region at that time also led to a dead end. Based on conversations with the Centers for Disease Control in Atlanta, Jake learned that the Mexican medical authorities had no obligation to provide any public health data to a private American citizen. Nor was the CDC willing to request the data unless he could persuade his local congressman to submit the request on his behalf. Jake was willing to go that route, but the CDC spokesperson warned him that Mexico was unlikely to reply in a timely fashion, if they ever did reply.

Finally, the July heat drove him out of his truck into his air-conditioned house. He spread the case folders out on the dining room table and started going through them one-by-one looking for some unturned stone, some avenue worth pursuing.

Looking at the clock he saw that it was almost time to prepare dinner. He turned to a blank piece of paper on a yellow pad and wrote his conclusions.

In the matter of Joanne Feldman's death he'd learned nothing that he didn't know seven years ago. In Betsy Lunsford's case, the trip to New Paltz to read the investigation report had yielded very little helpful information, and what it had yielded, seemingly, was impossible to follow up on. With regard to Angela Boyer, he had a theory but no way to either prove or disprove it.

"Why the long face?" Chloe Boyer asked when she arrived ten minutes late the next day for their mid-afternoon meeting at Spinelli's.

"I hate to admit it," Jake replied, "but we're no closer to pinning Angela's death on Bernard Johns than we were six weeks ago."

"But I thought you had a plan," Chloe stated.

"I did, but that plan has not yielded the smoking gun we need."

"I don't know what to say," Chloe said. "My grandmother is going to be very disappointed. She's put up a lot of money and you're saying you have nothing to show for it."

"To the contrary," Jake said. "We've learned a good deal. It's just that we still don't know two essential facts—how she contracted the disease and why neither her roommate nor Dr. Johns made any effort to get her medical attention. As far as the roommate is concerned, my guess is that she wasn't sleeping in the room and therefore can be excused from not knowing that Angela needed medical attention, but Dr. Johns knew she was ill and he didn't act. The problem is proving intent."

Chloe hesitated. "So you're giving up?"

"Not at all," Jake replied firmly. "But I'm running out of options. It would be different if I were a member of a police department. Then I could try to get a court order to look into a few things, but as of right now, we don't have enough to convince my former lieutenant to talk to a judge. I'll go over everything again. Maybe there's something I've overlooked."

"So why are we here?" Chloe demanded.

"You wanted to help," Jake reminded her. "This is what investigative work is like sometimes. You follow potential leads. Sometimes they help you uncover what took place, sometimes they turn out to be dead ends. You can't predict at the start where things will go. I thought we'd find enough to flush Johns out of the woods, and perhaps we have. That's my last gambit."

"What do you mean?"

"I'm close to asking Johns for an interview."

"And what if he says no?"

Jake shrugged. "He won't. That's tantamount to an admission of guilt."

Chloe put a pout on her face. "I wish you'd let me be there."

"You know I can't," Jake said.

"I know," Chloe answered. "I just wish I could do more to help."

"You've been great," Jake said. "I'll let you know how it goes. Meanwhile, call me if you think of something important."

16

Monday July 12: 12:30 p.m.

Jake was surprised to hear Chloe's voice on the phone two days after their meeting.

"What's up?" he asked.

"You said we needed to talk to Angela's girlfriends, right?"

"I did."

"Well, I just talked to Roxanne Miner, her best friend, and guess what?"

"Okay. I give up," Jake said.

"Right before the trip, when Roxanne called Angela to tell her about her mother's accident, Angela told her she might not be going, either. When Roxanne asked why, she said that she was breaking up with Dr. Johns."

"That is interesting. I'd like to talk to this Roxanne."

Chloe was silent for a moment. "What—you don't trust me?"

"It's not that at all, Chloe. That's good work on your part, but I need to hear her tell it to me so I can determine how good a witness she would be if we ever had to call on her to testify in court."

"Oh, well, in that case, here's her phone number." Chloe read off the number. "What's next?"

"I'll let you know after I've talked to her," Jake replied.

Roxanne Miner agreed to meet with Jake, but only if Chloe Boyer was present. Jake was not happy about that, but went along. They met at Spinelli's where their usual waitress, without being asked, brought Jake his coffee and Chloe her diet soda.

Jake wanted to get one thing out of the way at the start of the interview.

"Roxanne," he said, "what did you tell Angela when she told you that she was thinking of not going on the Mexico trip?"

Miner's face turned red. "Why are you asking me that?" she demanded. "I thought this was about Angela and the dentist."

"It is," Jake replied. "What did you tell her?"

Miner looked down at the table. "I told her to go," she said in a whisper.

"I suspected as much. Listen. You couldn't have known what would happen," Jake said. "It was what ninety-nine percent of people would have recommended."

"Still, she'd be alive today if—"

"Maybe. Or maybe she'd have gotten hit by a bus if she'd stayed home."

"That's not funny," Chloe said.

"Believe me. I'm not trying to be funny," Jake stated. "The fact is that Angela went and we would like to find out if she died needlessly. So, let's begin. Tell me about your conversation with Angela."

Miner told them that Angela had decided she did not see a future for herself with Dr. Johns and was waiting for the right opportunity to tell him. "He is so excited about the trip," Angela told her.

"What else did she say?" Jake asked.

"She didn't want to sleep with him any more."

"What were her exact words?"

Roxanne thought for a second. "She told me, 'I hate to ruin the trip, but I don't want to sleep with him on the trip.'"

"What did you say?"

"'You have to tell him in advance,' I told her. She said she would, but I don't know whether she did or didn't."

"Did she say why she didn't want to see Dr. Johns any more?" Jake asked.

"We'd talked about it more than once," Roxanne replied. "She liked him, but didn't love him. He was not 'Mr. Right.'"

"Was she worried about how he'd take it?"

"I guess so. When you have to tell someone it's over, they never expect it. Why is that?"

"You're asking the wrong guy," Jake replied. "Do you know if she'd tried to break it off before the trip?"

"Possibly," Roxanne said. "Do you know?" she asked, looking at Chloe.

"She didn't tell me if she did," Chloe answered.

"But you don't remember her saying that?" Jake asked.

"No. I suspect she did, but she never came out and said it."

"Did she seem afraid of him?" Jake asked Roxanne.

"No, not especially. I think she was mostly worried about ruining the trip for both of them."

"It's time to contact Dr. Johns," Jake told Chloe after Roxanne left the cafe, "but before I do, there's one more person I need to talk to."

"Who's that?"

"Dr. Johns' ex-wife."

"What does she know?"

"I'm not sure, but I'd like to know why she divorced him, for one," Jake said.

"That makes sense," Chloe replied.

"She's another base that needs to be touched before we call it a game. You never know when something will come up that helps the puzzle come together."

"Angela and I used to do jigsaw puzzles on rainy days when we were younger," Chloe volunteered. "I wanted to put the cover where I could see it, but she insisted we turn it over and figure it out ourselves."

"That's what we're doing," Jake said. "Putting together a puzzle without knowing what it will look like when it's done."

It took a few days and more than one dead end, but Jake finally found Phyllis Johns, Bernard Johns' ex-wife, living under her maiden name in a suburb of Phoenix. After explaining that her husband's name had come up in connection with the death of another Albany woman, she agreed to talk.

"When was the last time you spoke with your ex?" Jake began.

"It's been years. I let my lawyer do my talking."

"Have you received any correspondence from him?"

"Nothing. Dr. Johns and I are not on speaking terms. I told him seven years ago if he ever called me again, I would get a restraining order against him."

"Why was that?"

"After the divorce, he kept calling me at all hours of the day and night. Sometimes he'd beg me to take him back; sometimes he'd swear at me and call me a bitch. I told him our relationship was over and that he had to find someone else, but he kept calling. That's when I threatened to go to court."

"And after that, did he ever call you again?"

"I did get a number of suspicious phone calls. I'd answer the phone and no one was there. I suspected Bernard, but then the calls stopped."

Jake thought a minute. "When you lived in Albany, did you know an Angela Boyer?"

"Hmm. I recall the family name. Isn't her husband a lawyer?"

"Father."

"Sure. Well, I knew the name from the papers; I don't know if I ever met the man."

"So you never met the daughter, Angela?"

"I don't think so. How old was she?"

"Thirty-four."

"She's a bit younger than I am. It's unlikely we met."

"Okay. I'd like to go over a couple of your answers you gave seven years ago when my partner interviewed you in connection with the death of the attorney who had been dating your husband."

"That was ruled an accident, right?"

"Correct. You stated that you did not know Joanne Feldman, the victim."

"No, I did not."

"Did your ex ever talk to you about the women he was dating?"

"No."

"Does your ex have a problem with women?"

"Like what? I'm not sure what you're asking."

"You know. Some men dislike certain women—especially strong women who have minds of their own."

"I'm not a psychologist, Mr. Barnes."

"Your best guess. After your divorce, for example, do you think he viewed women in a different way?"

"It's possible."

"Let me ask you this. In your opinion, is Bernard Johns capable of murder?"

"Bernard Johns is capable of a lot of things that I don't think he'd be proud to have printed in the daily newspaper, but murder? No, he's too much of a coward to be a murderer."

"What do you mean?"

"I mean he doesn't stand up for himself. He lets some people walk all over him. That's part of what came between us. I wanted a man, not a mop."

"Did Dr. Johns ever threaten you with physical violence?"

"If he did, I didn't believe him."

"So your ex-husband did threaten you?"

"We argued a lot. He may have made vague threats, but if he'd have laid a hand on me, I'd have knocked every one of his precious teeth of out his pretty head."

"Did you ever fear that he would injure you?"

"Never. As I said, he's a coward at heart."

17

Monday, July 19: 1:45 p.m.

As instructed, Jake arrived a half an hour early for his two o'clock appointment with psychiatrist Dr. Martin Kreske. Jake recalled that Kreske had been a witness for the Albany County DA in an important case a few years ago and had handled himself well on the stand. He had tried to explain over the phone that he was a private investigator working on a case—not a patient—but it didn't matter to the woman with whom he made the appointment. "Come half an hour early," she insisted.

When he got to Dr. Kreske's office, he was given a set of forms to fill out and asked to produce his insurance information.

"I'm not here to see Dr. Kreske on a personal matter," Jake said in a hushed voice, given that there were several people in the waiting room of the plush offices in the multistory medical complex near the Albany Medical Center.

"Please fill out what you can," the receptionist replied, returning to her telephone conversation before Jake could protest further. He took the forms on the clipboard and found a seat. The form required family contact information, the name of the referring physician, and asked for a long list of health-related questions. He ignored all those and took the form back to the receptionist. She asked him to sign and date it at the bottom, which he did.

"The doctor will see you shortly," she informed him.

A nurse called for him ten minutes after two. "I need to get your weight and height," she said, leading him over to a scale. Given how conditioned the doctor's staff was to doing things their way, Jake realized that it would be futile to protest. He allowed her to add his measurements to the forms.

"This way," she said. She led him down a hall and knocked on a wooden door. She opened it without waiting for a reply, followed Jake into the room, and handed the clipboard with Jake's information to Dr. Kreske. The doctor was a tall pleasant-looking man, perhaps a few years younger than Jake. He came around his desk to shake Jake's hand and pointed to the couch next to a window whose blinds were closed, probably to hide a view of the parking garage.

Dr. Kreske sat down on the opposite side of a coffee table in a brown leather chair. He glanced through Jake's information quickly.

"How can I help you, Mr. Barnes?" he began. "Let me guess. You're dealing with impotency."

Jake was puzzled. "No. That's not it."

"No?" Dr. Kreske asked. "I thought the name. Jake Barnes. Impotency."

Jake laughed. "Not too many people make that connection, Doc. My given name is Robert, but a teacher started calling me 'Jake' after I turned in a very short English assignment. She asked me if I was striving to be the next Hemingway, and the name stuck."

Kreske chuckled.

"Of course, I had no idea who Ernest Hemingway was at the time, but I went to the library and found out."

"One of my favorite books," Dr. Kreske said. "Okay. If it's not for impotency, how can I help you?"

Jake took one of his business cards out of his shirt pocket and handed it to the doctor. "As I tried to explain to your receptionist, I'm here as a private investigator, Dr. Kreske, not as a patient. I am working on a case involving the death of a young woman that has been ruled accidental, but I believe there may have been foul play at work." He paused for a second to let that sink in. "There is a suspect who I believe has killed perhaps as many as three women. I was hoping that someone with your expertise could help me understand the suspect's motivation."

"I see. Well, I wish I'd known that was your agenda in advance."

"I did try to explain that to your receptionist," Jake said.

"Fine. Will I be asked to testify in court?" the doctor asked.

"Possibly," Jake replied.

"Because if I am, our state society has established a rate plan for expert testimony."

"At this point, I'm just trying to understand what's going on in this guy's head."

"I'm good at what I do, Mr. Barnes, but I'm not a mind reader."

"Touché," Jake said. "Let me provide you with a few details."

"Go ahead," the psychiatrist said, "but I'm not promising anything in advance."

"Understood. The suspect, whose name I won't divulge since you may know or have met him, is a forty-three-year-old male who is a respected member of his profession. He is divorced with no children. When I asked his wife why she divorced him eight years ago, she said that she was bored. She said he knew that she was looking for a certain lifestyle, which she described as active, involving travel and excitement. Instead, he turned out to be a low-energy type of guy, content to stay home and watch movies on TV."

"Sounds pretty normal to me," the doctor said with a smile.

"That's the background," Jake continued. "She divorces him and about eighteen months later, this guy is skiing with a woman that he has been dating and she goes off the edge of a cliff to her death."

"Tragic," the doctor said.

"Our suspect says it was her fault. She went past a warning sign and the ice gave way. He called her 'pushy.'"

"He could be right."

"The police department declared her death to be an accident. Case closed. Then, not quite four years later, another woman, who had been dating our suspect, fell off a cliff on a hiking trail down in New Paltz."

"Interesting. Was the suspect questioned?"

"He was not. The State Police concluded that the victim had been alone and that it was an accident or possibly suicide."

"Could be a coincidence. He seems to date woman who engage in risky behavior—skiing, hiking, and so on—activities where accidents do happen."

"So there's a pattern, right, to the kind of women he finds attractive?" Jake asked.

"That would be normal," Kreske replied. "It seems like you'd like to pin something on this guy, but you don't have any hard evidence. So you come to me looking for psychological evidence. But I'm sorry. From what you've told me thus far, I see a normal guy who needs to find a homebody for a mate."

"Okay," Jake said, "but here's the kicker. It happens again. Not the same MO, however. This time the woman he's been dating dies of spinal meningitis on a singles group trip to Mexico."

"Not most killers' choice of murder weapon."

"True, but this man is a medical professional and he is aware that she is sick, but he does not report that fact to anyone. Instead, he leaves her unattended and, by the time someone else finds her, she's too far gone to save."

"That is strange," Kreske admitted. "Are you certain he knew that she was that sick?"

"That information came to me from two of the suspect's friends who were on the trip."

"Curiouser and curiouser."

"So, you understand why I wanted to talk to you? I don't have any physical evidence, but three woman that this man dated are dead, and I can't help but think he's not the least bit sorry."

"Okay, I'm beginning to see your dilemma," Kreske said, "but I still don't have enough information to help you."

Jake shifted in his chair. "Try it this way, doc. What if the guy is sore about his wife ditching him, who, by the way, hit him up for some major bucks—he's got to be pretty angry, right? Perhaps he sees women like her as the source of his misery and he decides to get rid of them. Is anything like that possible?"

"Possible? Of course it is possible, but is it what happened? Who knows?"

"Don't angry people do vile and nasty things?"

"Sometimes. In most cases, however, they stop short of murder."

Jake nodded. "Understood."

"You have to understand how anger and violence work," Dr. Kreske stated. "Lots of people feel angry, but they don't become violent. In some cases, it is a matter of opportunity. People are angry with the government or with their employer, but they don't have the opportunity to do anything about those things. Most end up taking Tums while some of them spend time on my couch."

Jake nodded.

"Occasionally, though," Kreske continued, "the opportunity arises for a person who is carrying a lot of anger to get even. That may have happened in that first instance where the woman skied off the cliff."

"How so?" Jake asked.

"Say she did something to remind your suspect of his wife; then the opportunity presented itself for him to 'get even.' She skied out to the edge of the cliff and he thought, 'I'm boring eh? Try this for boring' and he pushes her off the cliff."

Jake smiled. "So the opportunity presented itself and he took advantage. Okay. Next: does he rat himself out or say it's an accident?"

"If that's how it happened, he feels justified. It was her doing, not his. He will claim she did it to herself."

"And then the second situation—could that also be considered a matter of opportunity?"

Kreske thought for a moment. "Perhaps. It is possible that it was premeditated, but you say he's a medical professional? If so, I can't imagine that he believes he's going to get away with the same story the second time. No, that one truly could have been an accident."

"No one even bothered to check if he had an alibi," Jake admitted.

"Too bad," Kreske said. "As to the third incidence, infecting someone with meningitis bacteria? How would he have obtained it; where did he keep it; how did he infect the victim with it? Too many questions to think it's anything more than an unfortunate coincidence."

"Okay," Jake said. "I'll grant you that there are some problems with that scenario, pinning it on my guy, but let's say each of these women in some way remind him of his wife and he feels vindicated in the first instance by having seized the opportunity to get rid of a pushy broad. Could he feel justified in planning the murders of the next two?"

"I think I've given you everything I can without actually talking to the suspect. You need physical evidence, but should you work from the idea that this person looks for opportunities to express his anger in that form? I find that an acceptable starting point."

"I'm about to interview the suspect. Is there some way I can tell if he's lying?"

"A lie detector?" They both laughed. "I'm sure you know," Dr. Kreske continued, "that lie detectors are not a hundred percent accurate."

"I do, plus I doubt he'd submit to one. Okay. How do you think he might he react if I push him hard—you, know, asked him directly if he killed these women?"

Dr. Kreske threw up his hands. "Who knows? In my opinion he's unlikely to break down and admit that he was responsible for the deaths of any of those women. Even if these accidents happened the way you suspect, he feels justified."

"How about if I use reverse psychology? I'll tell him some people think he's too timid to have done such a thing."

"Horrible expression, that."

"What?"

"Reverse psychology."

"I guess, but in any case, what kind of reaction do you think I'd get?"

"Interesting. In other words, you're taking the women's point of view. They see him as weak and ineffectual. He is compelled to prove them wrong. I'd be interested to learn how he reacts."

Jake thanked the doctor and was about to stand up when Dr. Kreske asked him a question.

"Mr. Barnes. I see here," he said, pointing to the form that Jake had filled out, "that you are recently widowed and that your daughter and grandson live with you. Is that correct?"

"Yes," Jake said.

"How long ago did your wife pass away?"

"It was last fall. November."

"I'm sorry to hear that. How long were you married?"

"Thirty-five years," Jake replied. He felt his chest constrict.

"It's good, then, that you are living with family and not alone."

"Yes, it has been good," Jake admitted.

"I also see that you are carrying some extra pounds."

Jake could feel his face redden. "I'm working on it," he said.

"Don't blame yourself, Mr. Barnes. It's hard to keep the pounds off during personal crises. Sometimes we have to complete the grieving process before we can work on our own issues. That can take a year or more."

Jake nodded. "I appreciate your saying so."

"It's good that you have your work to keep you busy," Dr. Kreske said, "but don't let your work interfere with the grieving process. Free advice from someone who sees a lot of patients who struggle long after a loved one dies because they postponed facing the loss head-on."

Jake spent time on the way home thinking more about the last minute of the conversation than about Dr. Johns. What did Dr. Kreske mean by 'grieving process'? No one had told him what to expect or how to deal with things after Margaret died. For weeks, he felt like the world had changed orbit. She had been ill for so long that they'd almost become comfortable with her being sick. On top of all that, Mary's marriage was on the rocks, which meant lots of drama as well as Mikey's spending time at their house. When Margaret passed and Mary told him she was getting a divorce, it seemed logical for her to move in with him. She could have stayed in their house, but decided to ask her ex-husband to sell it and give her half the proceeds. She used that money and the rest of the settlement to become a partner in the dress shop that she now managed.

Thinking back, Jake felt Mary's moving in had been a little rushed. He probably could have used a couple weeks to digest Margaret's passing; on the other hand, he was glad to have Mary's help going through his wife's clothes and things. He wouldn't have known, for example, what jewelry was worth something or how to deal with it. Some of it had come from her family. Mary kept a few items, but they sold most of it, using the proceeds to pay medical and funeral expenses.

Since then, Jake had taken to 'talking' to Margaret at various times during the day. Sometimes at night before he went to sleep, he'd go over his day as if she was sitting there, listening to him. Those conversations reminded Jake of how much over the years he'd relied on Margaret's common sense.

When he got home after the meeting with Dr. Kreske, Jake took Benji out for a long walk. He tried to put aside his thoughts about the grieving process and focus on the discussion about Dr. Johns.

He was still far from knowing where to go next, but at least now he felt he had a better understanding of what was motivating the man. Johns must have been angry about his divorce and Joanne Feldman had probably done something to bring back that feeling. Then, when she put herself in a position where Johns had the opportunity to do something, he acted. His ex had said over and over again that the man was passive. I guess he proved her wrong.

18

Tuesday, July 27: 6:30 p.m.

"What happened to Angela Boyer?" Jake asked Bernard Johns. They were sitting in the bar at the Omni Hotel in downtown Albany. Johns had refused to meet Jake at his office, insisting that he would only meet him in a public location. Jake had not been in a position to object and agreed to Johns' choice.

"We were told she died of meningitis. Other than that, I don't know what I can tell you."

"Do you know if she died of viral or bacterial meningitis?" Jake asked.

Johns gave Jake a stare. "I'm not sure," he stated finally.

"Do you have any idea how she came in contact with the disease?"

"Why are you asking me?" Johns replied. "You should be asking the Mexican medical authorities."

"Weren't you with her most of the time from the moment your group landed in Mexico?"

"We spent time together, but not twenty-four seven."

"Were you sick when you arrived in Mexico?"

Johns looked taken aback. "What's that got to do with anything?"

"But it's true, correct?"

"I was recovering from a case of the flu."

"What were you taking—an antibiotic?"

"For the flu? Rest and liquids is the recommended treatment."

"Was Angela Boyer ditching you?"

"Ditching me. Where'd you get that idea?"

"Humor me. Was she?"

"Not at all."

"That's not what her best friend, Roxanne Miner, says. She said Angela had told her that she was going to tell you no more sex and the relationship was over."

"She doesn't know what she's talking about," Johns said. "We never had any kind of exclusive deal in the first place."

"How long had you been dating?"

"About a year, I guess."

"That's a pretty long time in this day and age. Wouldn't you expect someone you'd put that much time into would reciprocate?"

"We had a good time together, but she wasn't ready to settle down."

"That seems to be your story, isn't it?"

"What do you mean?"

"You date these women who get tired of you after a while. Doesn't that piss you off?"

"I don't know what you're talking about. I'm doing fine playing the field."

"What happened to Betsy Lunsford?"

"Betsy Lunsford. What does she have to do with this?"

"You tell me."

"The New York police said she fell off a cliff," Johns said.

"Tell me about her," Jake said. "What kind of person was she?"

"She was not what she seemed," Dr. Johns said, warming to the subject. "She appeared to be all prim and proper, but she was pretty wild."

"Like what? She liked to party? Did drugs?"

"Both, but what she really was into was sex."

"Really!"

"As I said, it took me a while to find out, but while I was dating her, she was also sleeping with at least one other guy. And get this—once when she was tipsy, she bragged about having sex with a couple who lived in her building. She claimed they would call her up at odd moments, and if she wasn't busy, she'd go down to their apartment and they'd have a three-some."

"Did that bother you, her having sex with other people while she was dating you?"

Johns shifted in his seat. "I suppose it did a little at first. Made me wonder if I wasn't 'man' enough for her, but she kept telling me otherwise. She said she just had a bigger appetite than most people and I would have to accept that if I wanted to continue to see her."

"What about the other men? Did you ever meet any of them?"

"No. She mentioned one guy—an insurance executive, I believe. I gather he traveled quite a bit. That was why she joined the singles group, she told me. She didn't like sitting at home on Saturday nights."

"Anyone else?"

"Once we were at a restaurant and a man with a woman on his arm swung by our table and said hello. I got the vibe that they were, or had been, more than friends."

"Did she appear to have many women friends?"

"Not really; she definitely liked being with men."

"But to fall off a cliff like that! Wasn't she an experienced hiker?"

"Somewhat."

"How do you mean?"

Johns grinned. "Couldn't have been that experienced if she fell to her death."

"Is that what happened?"

"How would I know?"

"Perhaps someone pushed her."

"I don't know. I wasn't there."

"Just for fun. How might it have happened?" Jake asked.

"Hypothetically?"

Jake nodded.

Johns shrugged his shoulders, took a sip of his martini, and turned in his chair to face Jake. "I suppose she could have angered one of her boyfriends, told him she was moving on, and that pissed him off."

"Interesting. Describe what could have happened."

Johns was silent for a while. He started to speak a couple of times, but stopped himself. Finally, he spoke, leaning closer to Jake and lowering his voice.

"It could have happened like this. Say she had a date with someone, someone who was supposed to meet her at the Mohonk Mountain House. Have you ever been there?"

Jake shook his head.

"You should go sometime. It's a treasure. Excellent food, wonderful views, and they treat you right."

"I'll add it to my to-do list," Jake said.

Johns nodded. "Maybe she called her date and said she'd decided not to see him again. He might have gotten angry and cancelled then and there, told her he wasn't going to come on the hike. That makes sense, doesn't it? I mean, what self-respecting man would spend a weekend with a woman when she's just told him she was through with him?"

Johns drained his martini and motioned to the waiter for a refill.

"But say this man, who is pretty upset with being told that he's not up to her standards, decided at the last minute to have it out with her. But he couldn't appear to be angry. He had to make her believe that he was okay with her decision."

"Smart of him," Jake said.

"Exactly. So say he told her he'd meet her at the trailhead the next day. He couldn't drive his own car, of course, because someone might make note of its being there. But say he found another car and met her there with a smile on his face, like he was looking forward to the hike. You with me?"

Jake nodded.

"He'd wait until they reached a spot on the trail where no one else was around and confront her. She would get angry, which would make it easy for him to maneuver her over the edge. Then he'd return to his car and drive home. You know I'm only speculating here, making it up as I go along."

"Of course," Jake replied.

"That's how it could have happened . . . but I wouldn't know, since I was in Albany at the time."

"So you think it was the insurance guy?"

"Him, or maybe some other guy she was *shtupping*. That's the right word isn't it, *shtupping*?"

"Beats me, I'm Irish," Jake said. "So you were home in Albany all weekend?"

Johns nodded. "My car was in the garage for a warranty repair. I stayed home and watched football games all weekend—Notre Dame on Saturday and the Jets versus New England on Sunday."

"You remember the games that were on TV four years ago? Amazing."

"I know it was Notre Dame. It could have been the Bills against the Jets."

"You say you stayed home that weekend, but you could have rented a car, gone to New Paltz, pushed her over the edge, and then come back home," Jake suggested. "Earlier, you said the guy she'd broken up with wouldn't have gone there with his own car because someone might remember it. Why couldn't he have rented one instead?"

"I suppose he could have," Johns said, "but wouldn't the police be able to trace a rental, you know, if they had the tag?"

"Sure, and that would lead them to the killer. Too bad no one remembered any tags. Just one more question," Jake said. "Why would she have broken off with this guy? You just told me she had a healthy appetite for sex and she found him—shall we say—at least adequate."

"More than adequate, I would say," Johns answered. "Maybe he wasn't satisfied with being just another member of her harem. I suppose there's a word for a male harem, but I don't know what it is. Suppose he wanted exclusivity, but she wasn't ready to stop pretending that she was twenty-one? If he nagged her enough about it, she might have decided to break it off. That's just conjecture, of course. Who knows what women like her want? Their brains aren't like ours, Detective."

Johns finished off his martini and stood up suddenly. "It's getting late. This has been interesting, but I think I'll call it a night."

Jake watched Johns walk out of the hotel restaurant. He sat there for a while, feeling depressed. Johns had just told him how he'd killed Betsy Lunsford, but Jake couldn't see any way that he could prove it. He could try to get the records of the garage that serviced Johns' car. They would probably show the car was in the shop over that weekend. Then he could try to get car rental records. He wasn't sure if they were even available, but Johns had pretty much told him that he didn't rent the car he'd used. He sure didn't steal one. He could have borrowed one possibly, but from whom?

He needed a witness and Johns had said there'd been no witness. If someone had seen or heard her fall, wouldn't they have spoken up at the time?

In the matter of Angela Boyer, Johns had given him a lead. If he could prove that Johns was taking an antibiotic, that information would discredit his story that he was getting over the flu. By itself, however, it wouldn't be sufficient to prove that he had transmitted meningitis bacteria to Angela Boyer, but if he could prove Johns was taking an antibiotic, maybe he'd get Keller or someone to listen to him.

He ordered another beer. Dr. Johns was toying with him, confident that he had no way to prove that he had murdered any of three women. He thought he was safe.

Jake felt a headache coming on and his stomach was gurgling. It took every ounce of willpower not to stop for an ice cream. He turned on the TV when he got home, but couldn't find anything interesting to watch. He knew he'd toss and turn for a long time before falling asleep, but he had no remedy. Something has to give sooner or later, he thought. *Doesn't it?*

19

Wednesday, July 28: 10:15 a.m.

"Sorry, pal. You're on your own," Jake's former partner Ed Marshall told him.

He had called Ed to share the fact that Bernard Johns virtually told him how he'd killed Betsy Lunsford four years ago. The problem was how to prove it? Without a witness placing Johns at the scene, Ed argued, he'd need nothing less than a signed confession to be able to pin her death on him.

He hoped his former partner would be able to pick up on something that he'd missed. Ed more or less told him he was barking up a dead tree at a cardboard squirrel.

Given the chance, there were additional questions he'd like to ask Johns about Angela Boyer. Would he agree to undergo a second round of questioning? If he refused, what recourse did Jake have? His only hope was to come up with some evidence on one of the three cases that Johns would not be able to ignore.

Jake sat for a long time at his dining room table, going over the same pieces of paper. He felt more than stymied. There must be something else he could do to break the case open. Should he go to Mexico? What could he learn there? From the little he'd learned about meningitis, he knew that it was not rare for an American tourist to contract the disease, and that, from time to time, some of them died. Angela Boyer, a diabetes sufferer, could therefore be considered an unfortunate victim of a public health problem. The notion that she'd been infected deliberately seemed almost impossible to prove.

What about the fact that Bernard Johns had failed to help her get prompt medical attention? That would also be next to impossible to prove. To start, he'd have to convince people that Johns was responsible for Boyer's health because of their personal relationship; then he had to prove that he knew her illness was life-threatening. The chances of convincing a jury of both were less than slim.

In the end, Jake knew he had to accept the possibility that Johns would get away with his crimes. He was the perfect murderer—someone who was deemed to be a normal, productive member of his community whose apparent motive was not something that drove one in a million to commit murder. People get dumped all the time; usually they suck it up and move on.

Jake decided Benji needed a walk. It was a hot July day, so he kept to the shady side of the streets as much as possible. They walked slowly and aimlessly.

Halfway through the walk, Jake asked himself if the reason he couldn't find any solid evidence against Johns was because the man was innocent. Perhaps it was all in his imagination? Why was he trying so hard to prove that Bernard Johns was guilty? Was it to prove to himself and others that he'd been a good cop, a way of compensating for the way he'd been forced to retire?

He understood why some people might come to that conclusion. When he got home, he looked at himself in the mirror. He was still much too much overweight. He couldn't deny that his obsession with this case was bad for his health. Should he drop it and move on? At that point, he didn't have the answers to any of his questions.

That Tuesday was the Albany Singles Club's summer meeting. Jake had not planned on attending until Chloe Boyer called him with some interesting news.

"Word is, Dr. Johns has a new love interest," Chloe told him.

Jake decided to attend. He couldn't have said exactly why. The thought of Johns enjoying the company of another female companion made him angry. But what did he propose to do about it? He certainly couldn't bring up his suspicions to Johns' date. Johns would sue him and Jake knew he didn't have enough evidence to back up his claims in a court of law.

The singles club had moved the site of the meeting to a restaurant that had both inside and outside seating. As he walked toward the restaurant from where he'd parked his car, Jake suddenly felt awkward. What reason did he have for going, other than to spy on Bernard Johns? But he couldn't just stalk Johns for the next hour or two. He wasn't exactly prepared to be social. What would he talk about— the weather? That would last thirty seconds. Summer vacations? He'd yet to take one and had no plans to do so.

After signing in, Jake spotted Ellen Bartlett and Marlene Fitzpatrick standing next to a tall table with drinks in their hands. He purchased an O'Doul's from the bar and went over to say hello.

"Greetings, Detective," Ellen said. "How's your investigation going?"

"Good evening," Jake replied. "It's going."

"That's good," Marlene said. "Are you here to spy on a suspect?"

Jake pretended to be surprised. "Whoa! You got me," he said with a wink.

"We won't tell," she said. "Just tell us who it is and we'll keep an eye on him for you."

"Who's to say that it's a him?" Jake said.

"Touché," Ellen said. "I suppose a woman might have wanted Angela dead. She was beautiful, smart, and rich. Hard to compete against."

"Are you confessing?" Jake asked, winking a second time.

The women laughed.

"Maybe we knocked her off together," Marlene said winking back.

"I guess it's good that we can joke about it," Jake said. "Time has healed that wound a bit."

"I suppose so," Marlene said. "But I still think about her almost every day."

"So do I," Ellen stated.

"So, who is your suspect—Dr. Johns?" Marlene asked.

"What makes you think that?" Jake asked.

"He's the only person on the trip, other than us jealous women, who had a motive," she replied, giving Jake another wink.

"And what motive is that?" he inquired.

"He'd invested a lot of time in her," Ellen said. "If she didn't reciprocate, that might make him angry."

"Angry enough to kill her?" Jake asked.

"I guess that's what you're trying to find out," Ellen stated, munching on a caviar-topped cracker.

"He doesn't seem the type," Marlene said. "Not—I hate the term—macho enough."

Jake chuckled. He almost told them that Johns' wife had said the same thing.

"There's the good dentist now," Marlene said.

Jake turned to see Dr. Johns with a drink in his hand talking to Bill Parsons and a woman he didn't recognize.

"Who's the woman?" he asked.

"I don't know," Ellen replied. "Someone new. Want us to find out?"

"Thanks, but no thanks," Jake said.

"That's not stopping me," Marlene said. "I think I'll go over and introduce myself."

She wandered over to where Johns was standing. Ellen, perhaps so as not to abandon Jake, didn't follow. "So, are you a member of the club, Mr. Barnes, or just visiting?" she asked.

"I joined," Jake said. "I'm single."

"You were married?"

Jake nodded. "My wife passed away last fall."

"I'm sorry to hear that. Was it sudden?"

"Unfortunately, no. Uterine cancer. It took almost five years to kill her."

"How awful."

"You can't imagine," Jake said.

"But I'm sure she wouldn't want you to sit home and mope."

"Definitely not," Jake replied. "Not much chance of that, though."

"Oh?"

"My daughter and grandson moved in. They keep me from moping."

Ellen laughed. Marlene was on her way back to join them. "I got the scoop," she said. "Her name is Nancy

Marchand. She's with Met Life and she just relocated from Houston."

"Really?" Ellen stated. "Does she have a Southern accent?"

"She does," Marlene replied.

"Damn," Ellen said. "The boys will love that."

Jake noticed that Chloe Boyer had also made an appearance. They had discussed whether she should continue to avoid Jake at singles club meetings and agreed that she should not seem interested in talking to him and, especially, should not talk about the investigation. Jake nodded in Chloe's direction when she walked by on her way to the bar.

"So you know Angela's sister?" Marlene asked.

"I interviewed her a couple of times. She's interested in finding out what really happened."

"What really did happen?" Ellen asked. "What are the issues?"

"For starters, how did she contract the disease?" Jake asked.

Ellen shrugged. "Wouldn't you have to go to Mexico to find out?"

"Possibly," Jake replied.

"The trail must be pretty cold by now," Ellen said.

The conversation had gone as far as Jake felt comfortable. "I've monopolized your attention for too long, ladies," he stated. "It's been a pleasure talking to you."

"You too," Marlene said with a smile.

"Good luck," Ellen said.

Jake joined Chloe, who was standing at the bar talking to the club's president.

"Good evening, Mr. Barnes," Charlotte Richards said. "You know Chloe Boyer, I'm sure."

The three engaged in small talk while ordering their drinks. Richards seemed anxious to talk to Jake, as she continued to walk with him after Chloe wandered toward the food table.

"I hope you're not bothering people with your investigation, Mr. Barnes," Richards said. "This is a networking event and people need to feel free to come here and not be given the third degree."

"I understand," Jake said. "I'm off duty. I'm here as a single adult looking to make new friends."

"In that case, I don't have a problem. Enjoy yourself."

Peter G. Pollak

20

Sunday, August 15: 12:45 p.m.

July turned to August and, as the days went by, the heat of summer began to get old. Mary took Mikey off on their mother-and-son trip to Maine, leaving Jake to take care of Benji and the house. Frustrated over his inability to make any progress in his case against Bernard Johns, Jake tried to keep busy. He even went to the driving range a second time, but at the end of an hour, after hitting balls in every direction but straight, he decided to sell his golf clubs at the next neighborhood garage sale.

Things got so bad that during a brief phone conversation he had with Chloe, who made a habit of checking in with him once a week, he as much as admitted he was at a dead-end. "That doesn't mean the case is closed," he told her. "Sometimes you need to step away from an investigation to see it anew." He hoped she bought that argument, because he wasn't sure that he did.

Fortunately, she seemed to take the situation at face value. "You can keep calling me once a week," he said at the end of the conversation. She said she would. As a result, Jake was surprised to pick up the phone and hear her voice the following Sunday a little after midday.

"Nothing's changed," he started to say, but she interrupted him.

"I saw a blue Miata last night," Chloe said.

It took Jake a second to get his bearings. "Say that again."

"I saw a blue Miata. Didn't you tell me you were looking for one?"

"A blue Miata. Yes, I am looking for the owner of a specific 1999 blue Miata. Where did you see it?"

"I was out with Wilson, my current boyfriend. We were just arriving for dinner at Angelo's 677 Prime. You know where that is, I'm sure."

"On Broadway, right?"

"That's the one. So I had just gotten out of his car when the valet pulled up in a sapphire blue Miata. I waited to see whose car it was."

"And?"

"I didn't recognize the driver or his date, but I wrote down the license plate number."

"Good girl."

Jake wrote down the number and told Chloe he'd let her know what he found out. It was possible that the car was the wrong year and that its owner had nothing to do with Bernard Johns, but why not check it out? He didn't have anything else going at the moment.

The problem was that Jake didn't have access to the state's motor vehicle database, and he couldn't think of anyone on the Albany police force whom he wanted to ask a favor of. Not that there weren't four or five guys who would look up the information for him, but if it ever got back to Art Keller that they'd done so on his behalf, that person's career could be in jeopardy.

Finally, he had an idea. He looked up Curt Ellis in the phone book and dialed the number. Getting his answering machine, he left a message.

He stayed close to the telephone the rest of the day. He ate too much for lunch and afterwards sat on the couch watching a baseball game, feeling stuffed. Finally, at ten of seven that evening, as he was finishing eating a frozen dinner, the phone rang.

"Jake? It's Curt. What's up?"

"Thanks for calling me back, Curt. Listen, I need a favor. I need someone to check out a license plate for me, but the request can't be from me."

"All right. Give me some more information."

"The car may have a connection to the death of Betsy Lunsford. A blue 1999 Miata was seen in the parking lot of the trail where she died. But the State Police were never able to find the owner because they didn't have a plate to go by."

"So you're thinking if this is the car, the owner may know something about her death."

"Exactly."

"Okay. I've got someone in mind who might help. I'll let you know in a day or two."

Jake waited around his house all Monday and Tuesday, waiting for Ellis' phone call. It came late Tuesday afternoon.

"Does the name Shannon Lynch mean anything to you?"

"North side. Redhead. Decent street cop, right?"

"That's the one. She might be able to track the plate for you."

"Might?"

"She wants to meet you first to learn why you need the info," Ellis said. He explained that they'd have to meet after work. Jake often took Benji to a dog park a few blocks from his house. Could she meet him there at seven? Curt called back a while later confirming the meeting.

"I'll come too, if you don't mind," Ellis said.

"Not at all," Jake replied.

Benji was excited as they approached the dog park. If no other dogs were in the park, Jake would let him run around. Ellis showed up first.

"I'm not going to get dog shit on my shoes, am I?" he asked, hesitating at the gate. He was dressed in a stylish light blue suit with a white tie. His black shoes shined brightly.

"You never know," Jake said, holding the gate open.

Ellis tiptoed into the park and shoed Benji away when he tried to sniff him. Lynch drove up a few minutes later. Jake recognized her, just as he might any of the dozens of patrol officers with whom he'd interacted over the years. She must have changed after work because she was wearing tight black jeans and a black U-2 t-shirt.

She nodded to Ellis as she entered the dog park. Benji came up to investigate. "He's harmless," Jake said of the fox terrier. Lynch gave Benji a pat on the head. The dog must have decided she was okay because he went off to do more sniffing.

"I appreciate your help on this," Jake said. "The problem is that I'm not Lieutenant Keller's favorite ex-copper at the moment."

"I don't mind as long as I won't get burned," she said. "That's why I wanted to hear what you've got going."

Jake laughed. "No problem. Here's the story."

Lynch and Ellis listened without interruption as Jake reviewed the facts of his investigation in the death of Betsy Lunsford.

"So if it turns out that car has some connection to Dr. Johns, I think I can convince the State Police to reopen the investigation. As I said, no one ever questioned Johns about his whereabouts."

"I'm sure he has a ready alibi," Ellis said.

"Plus, given how long it's been, it's going to be hard checking out whatever story he tells them," Lynch added.

"Even so, it's all I've got."

"Okay. That's good enough for me," Lynch replied. She handed Jake a slip of paper. "The car belongs to a Richard Masthen. I wrote down the address."

Jake took the paper. His eyes lit up.

"Name ring a bell?" she asked.

"No, but the address does," he replied. "It's the address of the luxury condo that was built downtown a couple of years ago. Dr. Johns lives in that same building."

"Bingo!" Ellis said. "That can't be a coincidence!"

"That's an understatement," Jake said.

"Okay," Lynch said. "Listen. I've got to go. Keep me posted. I'm glad to help as long as I don't get in hot water."

"Thank you," Jake replied. "I owe you one."

"Wait," Ellis said to Lynch, "didn't you want to ask Jake something?"

She seemed to blush. "I didn't want to bother him."

"What bother?" Jake asked. "Tell me."

She kicked the dirt with her shoe. "I wondered . . . I mean, I thought . . ."

"Spit it out," Jake said. "I don't bite."

Lynch laughed. "It's just that I'm thinking of applying for your old job and I thought . . . Well, maybe that—"

"That I'd what?"

"You know. Tell me what you think of the idea?"

"You becoming a Detective. I think it's great. You've been on the force how many years?"

"Just nine."

"That's plenty. You've got a good record, right?"

"I guess so."

"Then what's the problem?"

"You know there's never been a female detective in the Albany PD."

"So? It's about time for that to change."

Lynch looked away. "I'm not sure I want to be the first."

"Why not? If you're qualified . . ."

"It's just that if I get the job, people are bound to say I got it because of affirmative action."

Jake shrugged his shoulders. "Aha. I suppose. But look, as you say, someone's got to be the first, and there will always be those who will bitch no matter who gets picked."

She nodded.

"Get the job and prove them wrong. That's all you can do."

She smiled. "Thanks."

"And if you don't get it this time they'll have to take you more seriously the next time."

"Makes sense," Lynch said.

"Absolutely," Jake said. "Get on their radar and, if you keep doing a good job, eventually they won't be able to pass you over."

She nodded.

"Tell me why you want this," Jake asked.

"I know I can do it. I work hard and I'm about helping people by getting the bad guys off the street."

"Okay," Jake said. "When they interview you, tell them that. Don't try to prettify it. Just be honest and straightforward. That's all you can do."

"Thanks, Jake. I really appreciate it."

"Good luck, kid."

She took off.

"Thanks, Curt. I owe you one," Jake said to Ellis.

"Glad to help."

"So, how do you know her?" Jake asked.

Ellis hesitated. "We went out for a while. I knew it wasn't a good idea—both of us on the job and one of us the wrong race."

"That's a heavy lift—even these days," Jake said.

"I got over that stuff years ago, man," Ellis said. "If I let that shit bother me, I'm as bad off as the bigots and racists."

"Good point."

"So what do you think about the car? This could be your big break, right?"

"Could be," Jake said. "If it turns out that this Richard Masthen loaned Bernard Johns his car on that particular Saturday, I'll go directly to the State Police."

"Not Art Keller?" Ellis asked.

"He wouldn't listen to me if smoke was pouring into his office and I told him the building was on fire."

"The state cops should go for it," Ellis conceded, "if you can put Johns at the scene of the crime."

"Exactly," Jake said.

"But what if it turns out that Masthen had the car that day? Maybe he went for a hike or was dating that gal, too?" Ellis asked.

"Shit! I didn't think of that. That would put an entirely different spin on the matter, wouldn't it?"

"I'm just saying be prepared for that to be the case."

Jake nodded. He would have to chew that one over in his mind for a while. "So you think I should call on this guy?"

"Sure, why not?"

"What if he won't meet me?"

"That tells you something right there. The State Police would surely want to talk to him if that were the case. You're good either way."

Jake nodded. He couldn't lose, but he planned to go to the public library first thing the next morning. He had to know who this guy was before he contacted him.

21

Wednesday, August 18 10:00 a.m.

It didn't take long for Jake to discover that Richard Masthen was a professor of English Literature at the University at Albany. He called the college switchboard and asked for Masthen's office number. A department secretary informed him that the fall semester hadn't started yet, which meant that Professor Masthen hadn't established his fall office hours. Not to be deterred, Jake drove over to the campus the next morning. After parking in a paid garage, he consulted a map of the campus and walked to the building where Masthen had an office on the third floor. The door was locked.

The building was mostly deserted. Jake walked up and down the corridor until he found a door that was ajar. He knocked and stuck his head in the door. "I'm looking for Richard Masthen. Any idea when he might be around?"

The occupant of the office was an elderly man sitting at a large desk in the midst of a pile of books. He stared at Jake over thick glasses. "Do I know you?" he asked.

"No," Jake replied. The old man shrugged, then picked up an electronic device and studied it for a few seconds.

"We've a department meeting Thursday morning at ten thirty," the man said. "He should be here then."

Jake thanked him and left, planning to return early Thursday morning.

Richard Masthen showed up at ten after ten that Thursday with two students trailing him. Jake knocked on the door after the students had gotten what they'd come for and left. Masthen, who had retreated behind his desk, didn't answer. Jake pushed the door open and stuck his head inside. "Professor Masthen?"

"Correct. What can I do for you?"

Jake stepped in and pulled his identification document out of his jacket. "I'm a private investigator working on the case of a mysterious death of a certain Betsy Lunsford four years ago. Does the name ring a bell?"

Masthen seemed taken aback. "Say that again," he requested.

"I'm investigating the circumstances surrounding the mysterious death four years ago of one Betsy Lunsford. Is the name familiar to you?"

Masthen shook his head. "Why are you asking me?"

"Because your nineteen ninety Miata was seen in the parking area at the foot of the Devil's Way Trail the morning Betsy Lunsford fell to her death."

"My Miata? Where? Where was this?"

"The twenty-first of October, nineteen ninety-five, down in Ulster County."

"Couldn't have been," Masthen stated. He looked at his watch. "Look. I have a meeting in five minutes Mr.— what did you say your name was?"

"Barnes. Jake Barnes. Why couldn't it have been your car?"

"Because I was in Ireland from the middle of August through the end of December doing research.

"Are you certain that it was nineteen-ninety-five?"

"Absolutely. I was in Dublin. So, sorry I can't help you, but as I said I've got a meeting—"

Jake interrupted. "Did you loan the car to anyone while you were away?"

"Loan my car? No, I didn't loan my car."

"You just left it in your garage for six months."

"Well, no. I left the keys with a friend so he could drive it around once a week to keep the tires from going flat."

"And the name of that friend is?"

"I'm not sure that I should convey that information to you, Mr. Barnes."

"Fine. If you'd prefer divulging the name to the New York State Police, I'll be glad to provide your contact information to them."

Masthen gave Jake a hard look. "I suppose that shines a different light on the matter, and it's not as if I have anything to hide. I left the keys with my neighbor, Dr. Bernard Johns."

It took Jake two days to get Melvin Lechansky, the New York State Police officer who had investigated Betsy Lunsford's death, on the phone. Lechansky remembered Jake's having spent a day reviewing their four-year-old file, but was only mildly interested to learn that Jake had found the owner of the 1990 Mazda Miata that had been in the parking lot at the foot of the Devil's Way Trail on that Sunday in October.

"So this guy gave the keys to his car to his neighbor and the car is the same make and color as the one described by the hiker," Lechansky said. "So what? The hiker didn't give us a license plate. He didn't even remember what state it was from. It's still a flimsy connection."

"Except for the fact that Dr. Bernard Johns, the man Richard Masthen entrusted his Miata with, told me hypothetically how Betsy Lunsford died. She could have been killed by a jilted boyfriend, he suggested, but he then claimed he couldn't have been the one because his car was in the shop. Isn't it worth investigating John's possible involvement given that he had access to Masthen's Miata, which matches the one that was described expertly by a man who was on that trail that day as having been in the parking lot at the foot of the trail? Why not ask Dr. Johns if he drove Richard Masthen's Miata to that trailhead, confronted Lunsford, and pushed her off the cliff?"

"I understand what you're saying," Lechansky said, "but so far all you've got is hearsay and conjecture."

"But isn't it enough to re-open the case? What harm could come from questioning Johns? Maybe he'd confess."

"Perhaps. It's not my decision, Mr. Barnes. I'll take your information to my captain, but I can't promise he'll look favorably on re-opening a four-year-old accidental death."

Jake took a deep breath. "I understand. There is one more piece of information to include when you present my information to your captain. Betsy Lunsford is not the only woman who died mysteriously while she was dating Bernard Johns."

"Well now, that could be a horse of a different color. Tell me more."

Jake described Johns' connection to Joanne Feldman and Angela Boyer.

"Taken one by one, pinning these deaths on this Dr. Johns is pretty weak, but when you consider that he's tied to all three . . . that's too much of a coincidence, if you ask me."

"Exactly," Jake replied.

"Okay, Barnes. I think I have enough to go on. I'll get back to you. It may take a few days."

"Not a problem. I've waited seven years. I can wait a few more days."

Jake tried to be patient over the next few days. He overcooked the dinner meatloaf Sunday night and left water running in the bathroom the following evening.

"Dad! When's the last time you had his hearing checked?" Mary asked him Monday evening.

"I don't know. Why do you ask?"

"I said 'good-night' twice," she answered.

He turned from the baseball game he'd been watching on the TV from the living room couch. "Sorry, I didn't hear you."

"That's what I mean," she replied, "and can you turn down the volume on that TV. You'll wake up Mikey."

Jake realized he didn't even know the score of the game. He'd been thinking how close he was to nailing Bernard Johns. He was convinced more than ever that Johns bore some guilt for all three deaths. Just one more nail in the coffin: that was all he needed.

Lechansky called two days later.

"Good news, Barnes," he said. "We're re-opening the case. The captain wants to find out how this guy reacts when we press him about the car."

"Excellent. He told me he spent the entire weekend at home. If you tell him that you have a witness who places Masthen's car in that parking lot, he's got to change his story."

"One would think so. I've got one more piece of good news."

"What's that?" Jake asked.

"I went through the entire file again myself and discovered that no one had bothered to check with the hotel as to how many people Lunsford reserved the room for. So I called them. It took a couple of hours for someone from their IT department to check it out, but he came up with the answer."

"Which is?"

"Which is that the initial reservation at the Mohonk House was for two people, but it was changed to one when Lunsford arrived. So, it looks like she had planned to spend the weekend with another person. Who could that have been? Most likely someone she was dating, and I'm sure we can find people who will testify that she'd been seeing your dentist."

Jake whistled. "Nice work."

"It's not the smoking gun, mind you, but if he's guilty, I think we've enough to make this guy nervous. Let's see how he responds. Perhaps he'll break when we catch him lying about having stayed home."

"By the way, will you be talking to any of the other people Lunsford was dating?"

"That seems like the prudent thing to do. Why?"

"Well, I've got the name of the man Lunsford was dating at the same time she was going out with Johns. He's married, which is undoubtedly why he wouldn't talk to me when I called him several months ago, but I'm sure you can persuade him to answer a few questions, including where he was on that day and did Lunsford ever talk about the other men she was dating."

"Not bad," Lechansky said. "What's his name and how do I find him?"

Jake gave Lechansky the information he had on Lunsford's insurance company friend.

"It'll take a few days for everything to be put in place," Lechansky said, "but we'll be coming over to talk to your Dr. Johns sooner rather than later. I'll let you know how it goes."

22

Thursday, September 9: 4:35 p.m.

Bernard Johns sat behind his desk, ignoring the flashing red light on his phone. He would answer it when he was good and ready; his receptionist knew better than to knock on the door. His computer screen told him that he had two more patients to see that afternoon. They must have been waiting quite a while. He could tell them to reschedule, but how would that look to his staff? No, he would calm himself down as if the grilling he'd just undergone was nothing important.

You did fine, he told himself. It was unfortunate that someone told the New York State Police that Richard Masthen's Miata had been seen in the parking lot by the Devil's Way Trail on the day nearly four years ago when Betsy Lunsford had fallen to her death. Nothing had come of it until now. Nothing until someone—Jake Barnes, undoubtedly—had uncovered the fact that Masthen had been in Europe and had entrusted his car to his keeping. Johns took refuge in the fact that the police had no physical evidence linking him to Betsy Lunsford's plunge. He had to admit that he'd been there, but they could not prove that the rest of his story was fiction.

Johns had started to sweat when his secretary announced that two New York State Police investigators wanted to see him. Perhaps it had something to do with one of his patients, he had thought hopefully, but when the investigators, whose names were Lechansky and Peccora, sat down in his office, the first thing they asked him was where he'd been on that October Saturday. There could only be one reason for them to question him after all this time. They had some reason to believe that he'd been in Ulster County.

"I drove down there to see if I could catch up with Ms. Lunsford before she started on her hike," he replied in answer to their initial question. "By the time I got there, her car was in the trailside parking lot, which meant she was already on the trail. I didn't know how big a lead she had on me, so I tried to catch up with her. But after hiking as fast as I could for an hour and not seeing any sign of her, I turned back and went home."

"Interesting," Officer Lechansky said. "Didn't you tell Jake Barnes that you'd spent the entire weekend at home?"

"I may have," Johns admitted.

"Why did you lie?"

"He seems to think I'm responsible for the deaths of a couple of women. It's absurd, but I didn't want to give him any information that would encourage him."

"So you admit that you lied to him?"

Johns nodded. "I suppose so."

"Describe your relationship with Ms. Lunsford," Officer Peccora asked.

"We'd been going out for a while. We enjoyed doing things together like skiing and hiking," Johns replied.

"How did you meet?"

"At the Albany Singles Club."

"And what were your plans for that weekend four years ago?" Lechansky asked.

"We had talked about doing a hike to see the fall foliage. She wanted to stay overnight and hike both Saturday and Sunday, but I wasn't up for hiking both days and wanted to stay local. She decided to go ahead without me. When I woke up Saturday morning, I changed my mind and decided I wanted to go and that I could get there before she started up the trail. My car was in the shop, so I took Professor Masthen's car. Unfortunately, I got there too late. She must have gotten up pretty early, went up the trail by herself, and you know the rest."

"What time did you leave Albany that morning?" Peccora asked.

"Let me think," Johns answered. "It must have been around seven." He knew she was going to hike the Devil's Way Trail, the hardest hike in that region. Because it was getting dark earlier each day, she planned to drive to the hotel Friday afternoon so she could be on the trail no later than nine Saturday morning.

Peccora wrote something down on his notepad. "Why didn't you call Lunsford to tell her you were coming?" he asked.

"I tried," Johns said, "but there was no answer."

"You tried her hotel room?"

"Yes, and her cell phone also."

"How long did it take you to get there?" Lechansky asked, taking over again.

"Under two hours."

"So, even though you hadn't been able to let her know you were coming, you drove two hours, parked, and then waited how long for her to show up?"

"Her car was already there when I arrived," Johns said. "So I started on the trail, but after an hour, I realized she had gotten too much of a head start and I'd never catch up."

"But if you'd kept going, wouldn't you have met her at the top or, at worst, when she started down?" Peccora asked.

"True, but that Devil's Way is not an easy trail, especially at the top, and, in my rush, I'd forgotten to bring any water or my walking sticks."

"So you went back down and left a note on her windshield?" Lechansky suggested.

"I went back down, but I didn't leave a note. I mean, what would the point have been?"

Lechansky looked surprised. "To let her know you'd driven all the way there to join her!"

"But I wasn't going to stay. Why let her know that I'd been there?" Johns said.

"I've got another scenario," Peccora interjected. "You got there before she did; you went up the trail and hid. When you saw her coming, you jumped out and pushed her over the edge."

Johns tried to keep his breath even and calm. He knew his face was flushed, but didn't think that was enough to hang him. "Now why would I do such a thing?" Johns asked, trying to force a smile.

"Because she told you she was ditching you," Peccora suggested.

"Where'd you get that?"

"Just answer the question."

"Not true, but even if she had, that's a pretty drastic reaction," Johns said. "What do you take me for?"

"Some people take rejection harder than others," Lechansky said.

"So, did she tell you she was through with you or not?" Peccora demanded.

"We were planning to spend the weekend together. Does that sound like she was, as you say, 'ditching' me?"

"Let us ask the questions, Dr. Johns."

Johns sat back in his chair. Lechansky looked down at his list of questions. "So you drove back to Albany. Then, did you try calling her that evening?"

"Actually, when I got back, I didn't have anything in the house for dinner, so I went out. By the time I got home, it was too late to call her."

"What hour was too late?"

"Nine, believe it or not. Hiking is very strenuous and I knew she'd be asleep by nine in order to get up early the next day for her second hike."

"When was she due back to Albany?"

"I'm not sure. She had talked about staying over Sunday so as not to have to drive after a long hike, but I don't know if that's what she intended to do."

"So, when did you try to call her?"

Johns thought for a minute. "I don't remember. That was four years ago. It might have been Monday night."

"What did you think when she didn't answer?"

"That she was out. I left a message."

"Did you try more than once?"

"I don't recall, but probably not. I figured I'd hear from her sooner or later."

"So you weren't concerned when she didn't call you back?"

"No, really. She was a very independent woman. Her work was demanding, often keeping her in the office evenings."

Peccora took over. "Dr. Johns, I still don't understand why you drove two hours to meet up with a person and then, when she wasn't there, you didn't make a greater effort to hook up with her. You could have gone over to the hotel where she was staying to wait for her and then hiked with her on Sunday, right?"

"True."

"So why didn't you?" Peccora demanded. "It was because you knew she wasn't coming down off the mountain, right?"

"Wrong. I didn't feel like waiting around all day for her to come back to the hotel. I'm not the kind of person who sits around all day waiting for someone. I decided to come back to Albany, where I had things to do."

"Like what?" Peccora asked.

"I had some paperwork to catch up on and I wanted to watch the Notre Dame game Saturday afternoon."

"So, you're a big football fan, I take it."

"I enjoy watching as much as the next guy."

"Apparently, the Mohonk Mountain House doesn't have any TVs," Peccora said, turning to his partner. He turned back to Johns waiting for a response.

"Is that a question?" Johns said.

Peccora nodded.

"I'm sure they do," Johns said, "but I don't see the relevance."

"My point is, you could have watched the game there."

"I suppose I could have, but I didn't choose to."

"I assume you and Ms. Lunsford were intimate?" Lechansky asked, taking over again.

"Did we have sex?" Johns replied. "Yes."

Lechansky leaned forward. "So, you didn't kill her because she wouldn't sleep with you?"

Johns decided it was okay to show that their questions were annoying. "I didn't kill her, period," he replied in as convincing a voice as he could muster.

"If I had asked you at the time whether she was your girlfriend, what would you have said?"

"We were both beyond the ages of playing boy friend and girlfriend," Johns answered. "I would have said we were friends, period."

"Were you dating anyone else at the time?" Peccora asked.

"We weren't exclusive, if that's what you want to know."

"Who else were you going out with that fall?"

Johns hesitated. "Isn't that my business?"

"We're just trying to verify what you're telling us, Dr. Johns," Peccora stated. "You can help yourself by cooperating. Names and contact information, please."

"I don't keep personal information in my office," Johns stated.

"Just names, then."

"There was Susan Willingham, for one."

"She lives in Albany?"

"Yes."

"What does she do?"

"She's a research tech at Albany Med."

"When's the last time you went out with her?"

"A year or two ago. I haven't seen her in a while."

"Anyone else?"

"I probably went out with several different people, but I don't keep their names on a spreadsheet."

"Tell us about your first wife," Lechansky said.

"Not much to tell," Johns replied. "We got married young. It didn't work out."

"The divorce was amiable?"

"More or less."

"Tell us about the less."

"Her lawyer asked for a lot more than she deserved, considering she never worked a day in her life."

"Who asked for the divorce?" Peccora asked.

"I don't recall," Johns replied.

"We can look it up to refresh your memory."

Johns winced. That implied that they might come back. "She initiated it, but I didn't object."

"Why didn't you come forward when Betsy Lunsford's body was discovered?" Peccora asked.

"What good would that have done?"

"If you were innocent, it would have helped us get answers sooner. Perhaps you didn't come forward because you would have been questioned about your whereabouts and, when we found out that you'd been on the trail, that might have made you a suspect, right?"

"I don't see how."

"If you'd told us that you'd been there, but didn't stay, we'd have asked a lot of questions, ones that might have been hard for you to answer."

"Not really," Johns said.

"So you were protecting yourself, which, to me, suggests that you felt guilty about something then, and still feel guilty today. Am I right?"

Johns shrugged. "I suppose I thought if I'd gone with her that weekend, she'd still be alive."

"That's not what I had in mind," Peccora replied.

"Then I'm not sure what you're driving at."

"Let me try, Dr. Johns," Lechansky stated. "If you were innocent, you would have done the honorable thing in contacting us and telling us about your attempt to meet up with Ms. Lunsford. But a guilty person will do anything and everything possible to keep from being looked at a suspect."

"You guys are the experts."

"That's right," Lechansky said. "So, let me give you one more chance to tell us the truth, because we're not done here. What really happened on the twenty-first of October, nineteen ninety-five?"

"I've already told you what I did that day. What more can I do?"

"Stop playing games," Peccora stated.

"I'm sorry, gentlemen, but if you have no more questions, I do have patients waiting to see me."

They left, promising that he'd hear from them again soon.

23

Same Day: 5:45 p.m.

"Whew, she's not home," Bernard Johns said to himself. He left a message on Nancy Marchand's home phone cancelling their date for that evening, claiming a headache. He didn't think he could pull off the devil-may-care attitude he put on in her company. He needed time to reflect on what he could expect from the State Police. He had to be better prepared if and when they came back.

When he got into his car, he realized he didn't want to go home, nor was he particularly hungry. "Go for a drive," he told himself.

An hour later he found himself in Thatcher Park. There were too many cars at the lookout parking area, so he drove up to the last picnic area, parked his car, and started wandering up the hill. He walked slowly as the late afternoon August heat had not yet dissipated.

After walking for fifteen minutes, he realized he was at the very spot where he'd pushed Joanne Feldman off the cliff. *Why did I come here?*

He was about to turn around and head back down the hill when someone called his name.

"Dr. Johns—is that you?"

He looked around. "Damn," he said to himself. It's Chloe Boyer. She was coming toward him from a table where a group of people seemed to be having a cookout. She was wearing shorts—very tight shorts and a tank top. He'd always thought of her as a teenager, but she must be at least twenty-two or twenty-three.

"Hi, Chloe," Johns said putting on the best friendly face he could muster.

"Dr. Johns, what are you doing up here?" Chloe asked when she got closer.

"I thought it would be cooler than staying in the city. How about yourself?"

"Oh, I'm with a group of friends from high school—Girls' and Boys' Academy grads."

Johns started walking down the hill. "That's nice. Well, I was just about to head back to the city. So have a nice time."

"Before you go, could I ask you something?"

Johns let out a sigh. *Now what?*

Chloe started walking with him. "About Angela. How did you not recognize that she was so sick?"

Johns tried to keep his emotions in check. He wanted to scream at her. To tell her he didn't kill her sister, but that would likely backfire—make her more convinced that he had more to do with Angela's death than he did.

"I'm glad you asked about that, Chloe," he said after gaining his composure. "As long as it won't upset you too much by going over what happened?"

Chloe shook her head. "I'm a big girl. I can take it."

"Okay," Johns said. "It started when she didn't show up to dinner one night. One of her women friends went to her room to see if she was all right. The woman came back and told us that she was skipping dinner because she wasn't feeling well. Some of us had experienced stomach issues on the trip. We thought that was it."

Johns tried not to be distracted by Chloe's facial reactions as he talked. She seemed on the verge of crying. "Should I continue?"

Chloe nodded.

"The next day, a few of us were planning a trip into town to do some shopping—gifts for friends and family. The main group went to some ruins. I'd seen enough ruins for one trip and some others agreed. I went to Angela's room to see if she wanted to join us, because she wasn't at breakfast. I knocked on the door. She opened it just a crack and told me she didn't feel up to coming along. I asked her if I should tell the tour leader that she was sick. She shook her head and said she'd probably be fine by dinner."

Chloe turned away to wipe a tear from her face. Johns waited. "I'm okay," she said.

Johns tried to give her an encouraging smile. His conversation with Angela hadn't gone exactly like he was telling it, but who would ever know? "When we got back late that afternoon, I thought of checking up on her, but I ran into the woman she was rooming with—Karen, I think her name is. I asked her how Angela was feeling and she said she was sleeping the last time she checked. So, I thought everything was fine and went to my room to rest before dinner. Later, I guess one of Angela's friends asked the roommate to let her into the room. That's when they discovered she wasn't doing well and contacted Dr. Smythe who decided she needed to go to the hospital."

Johns paused. Chloe's face was red. He couldn't tell if it was due to the tears or anger.

"That's it?" she asked.

"It's a terrible disease, Chloe. It acted so fast. We were all terribly upset—me especially, because we'd been so—"

"You should have insisted. You should have told the tour director. You should have done something!"

"I don't think anyone else would have—"

"But you're a doctor."

"Yes, but not that kind."

"But you're trained, aren't you, to recognize when someone has a stomach virus or is dying?"

"Chloe, I only saw her through a crack in the door. She didn't let me—"

"Someone should have—"

"You're just upsetting yourself. What's to be gained by going over it again and again?" Johns resumed walking down the hill.

"She wasn't the first, was she?"

Johns stopped and turned back. "What do you mean?"

"She wasn't the first of your girlfriends to die a strange death."

Johns went back to where Chloe was standing. "Have you been talking to that crazy detective? I don't know what I did that made him think I'm some kind of murderer, but you can't go around accusing people of doing things when you don't have any evidence."

"You can't get away with it forever," Chloe said. "He's going to find some evidence and you're going to prison."

"I think I've put up with as much of this as I need to. I'm leaving. Go back to your friends. I'm sorry Angela got sick, but I didn't have anything to do with it, and you'll only make yourself sick if you keep harping on it."

Johns turned and walked quickly back down the hill. He was sweating heavily by the time he reached his car. "Damn that Jake Barnes," he said to himself. *It's all his fault. The*

State Police earlier today. Now that crazy girl. I'm not going to take this lying down. He's going to pay.

24

Monday, September 13: 10:15 a.m.

Jake picked up the phone on the third ring.

"Mr. Barnes. This is Bernard Johns."

Jake wasn't sure he'd heard correctly. "Say again?"

"Bernard Johns. You know? Your favorite dentist."

"Hello, Dr. Johns. What can I do for you?"

"You can meet me tomorrow at noon in the upper parking lot in Thatcher Park."

"Okay," Jake replied. "Is there a particular reason you want to meet there?"

"I'm tired of being accused of killing these women. I want to take you back to the spot where Joanne Feldman fell to show you that I was not responsible."

Jake hesitated for a few seconds. "Okay. I'll listen to what you have to say."

"Good. I'll see you then."

Jake held the phone to his ear long after Johns hung up on him. He finally put it down rubbed his face with his hands. *What in the world?*

He sat down, trying to figure out what Johns was up to and how he should play it. The first thing he decided to do was call Officer Lechansky of the New York State Police.

Lechansky was out, so Jake left a message. He thought about calling Art Keller, but instead put in a call to Curt Ellis at his office. Ellis was also out.

Lechansky called back a couple of hours later.

"Very interesting," he said. "I don't think it's a coincidence that he called you a day after we visited him."

"How'd that go?" Jake asked.

"As good as could be expected," Lechansky replied. "He admitted lying to you and the rest of his story doesn't hold water, but he's very crafty. We're going to keep working on this."

"What's next?"

"We're going to revisit the scene. I'm waiting to hear from an expert who can help us determine the place on the trail where she fell. Maybe if I ask Johns about that location, he'll say something that proves he was there."

"So you're going to question him again?"

"No doubt. When you meet with him, ask him about the interview so he knows you know that we're looking at him. Let me know how he reacts."

Curt Ellis didn't call until that evening.

"I need your advice on how to handle a situation," Jake told him.

"I'll do what I can," Ellis replied.

"I got a call from Dr. Johns earlier today. He wants me to meet him tomorrow morning in Thatcher Park."

"Interesting. Did he say why?"

"He did. He wants to go over how Joanne Feldman fell off that cliff seven years ago."

"Why now, do you think?"

"Because thanks to me, he's getting heat from the New York State Police on another death that occurred four years ago."

"So he thinks you'll lay off if he can convince you that this Feldman's death was accidental."

"I think that's what he wants me to believe."

"But you're not certain?"

"I'm not. I hate to admit it, but the guy's a mystery to me."

"Well. I'd go, but I'd be on my toes the whole time."

"Will do, but here's my question. Should I tell Keller?"

"I don't see why. He's got enough on his mind these days."

"Okay," Jake said. "I suppose I can call Keller later if he tells me something significant."

"What about wearing a wire?" Ellis suggested. "That way Johns can't dispute later on what he tells you."

"Good suggestion. I'm surprised he didn't mention that. He didn't even tell me to come alone."

"Probably thought that would look suspicious."

"You could be right," Jake said. "As I said, the guy's hard to figure."

"Let me know how it turns out," Ellis said.

"Will do."

When he hung up, Jake noticed that his daughter had taken an interest in the conversation.

"What's going on, Dad?" she asked.

"Dr. Johns. He wants to talk to me about the case I investigated seven years ago, the one where the woman plunged off a cliff on skis."

"Why now after all this time? Do you think he's going to admit that he pushed her?"

"I'd be shocked if he did. I think he wants to try to convince me he's innocent so I'll lay off him on the other two cases."

"Are you going to go?"

"Sure. Got to."

"Bring someone along."

"If I do, he's less likely to say what he's got to say."

"But what if he brings a gun?"

"I don't think he's that stupid. Right now we're making him feel uncomfortable, but we don't have any hard evidence. He'd be crazy to do something like that."

"Maybe he is crazy," Mary said.

"You've never met the guy, but he tries to be this very cool, cosmopolitan person. He probably believes that we don't have enough to convict him if he doesn't do anything to blow his cover, but I'll take my Sig if it makes you feel less anxious."

"Is that the little one you taught me to shoot?"

"Yup—the P232—small and light, but very accurate at close range."

"Still, be careful, will you, Dad?"

"Of course. I'll tell him right away that several people know that I'm meeting with him, which is true. I might even say I told the head of detectives. So, even if he has any funny ideas, that should dissuade him from acting on them. Second, he's too weak to try anything physical on me. No, I think he thinks he can outsmart me."

"I'm still going to be nervous until I hear from you. Call me as soon as your little meeting with him is over."

"Will do."

Late that afternoon, Jake got a call from Chloe Boyer.

"I'm calling to cheer you up," she said.

"That's nice of you," Jake replied. "Got some good news to tell me?"

"I do," she replied. "I'm engaged."

"Really. That's terrific. Who's the lucky guy?"

"His name is Wilson Hernandez. He's an Albany Assistant DA. Very smart and he's cute, too."

"I'll bet. That should please your parents."

"My mother's excited, but I knew she would be. She's been worried about me. My father surprised me. I was worried because Wilson's parents are from Puerto Rico, but Daddy's been very gracious and told me I could have whatever kind of wedding I wanted."

"Wonderful."

"And what about you, Mr. Barnes? Are you still working on my sister's case?"

Jake hesitated. "In a sense, I am, but the focus has shifted to the death of Betsy Lunsford in October 1995."

"Really! Did my telling you about that car help?"

"It did. That might have been the snowflake that started the avalanche that will put Dr. Johns behind bars."

"I'm so glad. Can you tell me any of the details?"

"Only this—the New York State Police have re-opened their investigation and Dr. Johns is very nervous."

"Do you think he'll confess?"

"I wouldn't hold my breath, although I'm going to give him a chance to do so tomorrow."

"What do you mean?"

"He asked to meet with me. He says that he wants to prove why he didn't kill Joanne Feldman."

"He didn't say anything about Angela?"

"No, I'm sorry, Chloe. He didn't."

"Where are you meeting him? The Omni again?"

"No, in Thatcher Park. He says it has to do with where Joanne Feldman fell to her death."

"Thatcher Park! I saw him there a couple of days ago."

Jake was taken aback. "You're kidding?"

"Nope. I was picnicking with some friends and I saw him standing by the edge looking out over the cliff. Even though it was still pretty warm, he was wearing a suit and tie."

"Did you talk to him?" Jake asked.

"I did. I'm afraid I lit into him for not telling someone that Angela was so sick."

"How did he react?"

"It upset him, but he denied he could have done anything. I even asked him about those other women."

"Holy cow! What did he say?"

"He accused me of listening to you and walked away."

"Very interesting. We're getting to him. That must be why he called me. He must think he can slow down the investigation somehow."

"Are you going alone?"

"I was planning to."

"I don't trust him. People have a habit of dying in his company."

"Don't I know it! Tell you what. I can use your help. Are you free tomorrow?"

25

Tuesday, September 15: Noon

Tuesday broke like a typical fall day. It had dropped below sixty degrees overnight, but the sun was out and promised to warm things up. Jake put his service revolver in the glove compartment of his pickup and headed for his rendezvous with Bernard Johns. He stopped at the Stewart's Shop on New Scotland Avenue and filled up his gas tank while waiting for Chloe to show up. Having consumed two and a half cups of coffee that morning, he went inside to get a bottle of water. He didn't need to make himself any more jittery than he already was.

When Chloe arrived, he gave her an earpiece from the dual band radio set he'd purchased some years ago. Before he left home, he had secured the tiny microphone to the collar of his jacket and strapped the radio transmitter behind his back under his shirt.

"You should be able to hear everything I say and, unless Dr. Johns stands too far away from me, you'll hear him, also. When you get to the parking lot, make sure you have service for your cell phone. That way if he tries something funny, call nine-one-one right away."

To test the system, he drove a few blocks farther east in the direction of Thatcher Park, then pulled over to the side of the road.

"Call me on my cell if you can hear me, okay?" he said at a normal voice level.

A minute later his cell phone rang. It was Chloe. "I heard you plain and clear."

"Good. Be sure to park in the lower lot until you see Dr. Johns' Caddy go by. Then wait five minutes and drive up to where we're parked. He wants to meet me at the highest lot in the park. You should be able to hear us the entire time. When it's obvious that we're on the way back to our cars, drive down one lot and pull in. Duck down so he doesn't see you when he drives by. I'll find you and we can compare notes."

"But if he pulls a gun on you, won't calling nine-one-one be too late?"

"It's extremely unlikely he'll do something that stupid," Jake replied. "He's been Mr. Cool Customer up-to-now. He thinks he's smarter than the rest of us, but just in case he gets out of line, I've got a back-up pistol and I'll be ready for him."

After Chloe affirmed that she knew what to do, Jake headed toward the parking lot where he was to meet Dr. Johns. He knew that it would not be good if Johns was already there waiting for him, suggesting he had set up something in advance. But forty-five minutes later, he was pleasantly surprised when he pulled into the farthest parking area in the state park. There was only one car in the lot and Johns' Cadillac was not to be seen.

Jake got out of his truck and sat on a nearby picnic table drinking his water, waiting. It was ten after noon before Dr. Johns drove up.

"Sorry, I'm late," Johns called, getting out of his car. "I thought I'd pick up a couple of sandwiches and some coffee." He displayed a see-through bag with a Subway logo on it. "What I want to show you is about twenty minutes up the hill."

"After you," Jake said.

They walked in silence. The trees had just started turning. There was a smell of fall in the air. Jake was sweating after only a few minutes walking up the trail. I'm still not exercising enough, he told himself. He had lost five pounds earlier in the summer, but lately had fallen off the dieting wagon.

I'm going to start a new regime tomorrow, he swore to himself. What had prevented him from signing up at one of the area gyms was the thought of his body sticking out like the aging, fat, ex-cop that he was in the same room with all those young in-shape people. *That can't be helped.* I'll join the Y, he promised himself.

A few minutes later Jake had to stop to catch his breath. He pretended to be looking at the view.

"The view's even better higher up," Johns told him.

Wipe that smirk off your face, Jake wanted to say to the younger man, but he restrained himself.

Jake was breathing heavily when Johns stopped at a spot where visitors could go to the edge of the cliff for an open view of the valley below. The Albany skyline stood out in the distance.

There was a guardrail and a sign warning people of the danger. "That's where it happened," Johns said. "I haven't been back here since that day."

Liar! Jake almost said aloud. This must have been was he was standing when Chloe had spotted him the previous week. "So, is that what you wanted to tell me?"

"I wanted to explain why I couldn't have killed Joanne Feldman. I have a fear of heights," Dr. Johns said, stopping ten yards short of the guardrail. "The guardrail was covered by snow. So you could go right to the edge. That's what she did, but I wouldn't go near it."

Jake walked to the edge. What a view, he told himself, until he looked down and saw the treetops and ragged rocks that must have broken Feldman's fall. He stood sideways, half-expecting Johns to run at him and try to push him over the edge. "So that's your proof—that you have a fear of heights?"

Johns nodded. "I can't come any closer than I am now."

"But you weren't sorry to see her go, right?"

"You're always casting me in the worst light, Barnes."

"I'm just looking for the truth, Dr. Johns."

Johns pointed to some picnic tables further up the trail. "Let's sit and have a bite."

Jake thought about turning him down, but he wanted to push Johns further. So he went along.

Johns put the bag containing the sandwiches on one of the tables. "Wasn't sure what you like. I got one tuna sub and one Italian cold-cut combo. You take milk in your coffee, right?"

Jake took the tuna because he thought Johns would have figured that he'd choose the cold cuts. Johns sat down and started on his sandwich.

Jake wanted to sniff the coffee, but that would be too obvious. He took a small bite of the sandwich instead. "So, that's it? That's why we're up here?"

"I thought if I made an effort to explain that to you that you'd stop this silly game you're playing."

Jake took another bite of the sandwich.

"I also wanted you to know that I didn't appreciate being grilled by the New York State Police about Betsy Lunsford," Johns said.

Now we're getting someplace. "They're just doing their job. For some reason they seem to think you were at the trailhead down in Ulster County the day she went over the cliff."

"I was there."

"That's not what you told me," Jake said.

"I was tired of your harassing me about these women. I lied. So there. I'm human."

"So, why did you go there?"

"As I told them, I changed my mind about the weekend, but she'd already gone up the trail by the time I got there," Johns stated. "So I drove home."

"They buy that?"

"They didn't have any choice, Barnes, because they don't have any physical evidence tying me to Lunsford's death."

Jake shook his head. "So you think you're going to get away with having murdered Betsy Lunsford?"

"You told them about our discussion, our hypothetical discussion?" Johns accused.

"Of course I did," Jake replied. "You told me how you killed her."

"How someone might have killed her. I didn't say that I was the one."

"But you're admitting she was pushed."

"No, I'm not admitting anything."

"How's it going with this new dame, Nancy Marchand?"

"Fine, we've gone out a couple of times."

"You sleep with her?"

"I am not going to answer that question, Barnes."

"In other words, you struck out again!"

"That's not a very nice way of putting it, Barnes," Johns said, grimacing.

Jake wasn't placated. "So, what happens now, Doctor? When will Nancy suffer an unfortunate accident?"

"All accidents are unfortunate, Mr. Barnes, and I resent your continued unfounded accusations. I thought we could talk like grown-ups. Perhaps I was mistaken."

"We are talking like grown-ups," Jake retorted, taking a sip of the coffee. "I'm pointing out that if the pattern holds true, Nancy Marchand is in mortal danger."

"So you think bad luck is contagious." Johns said, chuckling.

Jake didn't laugh. "You're not funny, Doctor," he stated. "Three young women met their untimely demise after having met and dated you. That's more than bad luck."

"You're wrong," Johns said. "I got along fabulously with all three. Joanne Feldman and I got along fine, and, as I told you, Betsy Lunsford and I were having great sex."

"One of Lunsford's girlfriends told me that she was planning on telling you not to call her any more," Jake said.

"Hearsay," Johns replied.

Jake took another sip of the coffee. "If things were so great, then why'd you kill her?"

Johns frowned. "You don't give up do you?"

"Not when there's no other reasonable explanation. And what about Angela Boyer?" Jake asked. "I know she was calling it off."

"More hearsay," Johns stated. "Things were going quite well between us until she got sick and died of spinal meningitis."

"How did you feel about that?" Jake asked.

"Devastated, of course. I still can't believe it. She was a wonderful young woman—"

"Who wasn't ready to settle for a divorced dentist. Was that the rub?"

Johns looked like his feelings had been hurt. "She was not the type of person to judge others by superficial qualities."

"One's profession is hardly superficial," Jake said. He took another sip of the coffee as Johns took a bite of his sandwich. This is the most bizarre situation I've ever been in, Jake thought. *I'm arguing with a psychopathic killer.* There was little to be gained. Johns would never admit that he'd done what he'd done, probably because he couldn't admit the truth to himself.

"You know, I've taken about all the accusations I'm going to take," Johns said, interrupting Jake's musings. "If you don't stop, I'm going to sue you for defamation of character."

"Is that a threat or a promise?" Jake replied.

"Childish taunts will not protect you, Mr. Barnes. Either put up the evidence or shut up and get on with your life."

Jake stared at the man. He had to admit that he had balls.

"You know, Barnes, you ought to consider the impact losing a suit would have on your daughter's business and on your grandson."

"What do you know about them?" Jake demanded standing up.

Johns got up and backed away from the table. "I know that your wife passed away about a year ago and that you had to retire from the police force due to health problems," Johns said. "If I had your blood pressure, I'd find something to do with my life other than harassing private citizens."

All of a sudden, Jake felt light-headed, as if Johns' words had triggered something in his body. He grabbed the edge of the table to keep from falling and lowered himself back onto the picnic table bench.

"Maybe my warning came too late," Johns said with smirk on his face.

"What?" Jake mumbled. Johns seemed to have split into two bodies. He rubbed his eyes. "What's happening?"

"You seemed to have overexerted yourself," Johns said.

Jake felt his heart beating rapidly in his chest. He needed to call 911. Where was Chloe? Another wave of dizziness passed through his body, causing him to grab the table again. He had all he could do to keep from falling off the bench. "What did you . . . ?"

"Nothing, really," Johns replied. "You just drank a little something to make your heart work a little harder." He smirked and took a step back toward the table. "Why not take another sip of coffee, Jake? It'll make you feel better."

"Shut up," Jake said. He pulled his cell phone out of his pocket and tried to dial 911.

"It won't work from here, Barnes," Johns said. "I tested that out before I picked this location."

"You bastard."

"That's good. Get angry, Jake. Get real angry."

Jake held the phone to his ear. No signal. Another wave of dizziness caused him to put his head in his arms. He looked up. Where is Chloe?

"Goodbye, Jake," Johns said. "I'm sorry I can't stay here to see your final minutes. Have a nice death."

Jake's head was swimming as he watched Johns pick up the remains of his sandwich, pour the rest of his coffee on the ground, and stuff the cups and the remains of the sandwiches into the Subway bag. He tried to turn around to follow Johns as he walked back down the trail, but the movement caused him to lose his balance and he fell off the bench onto the ground. Then everything went black.

26

Same Day: 9:15 p.m.

"You're the daughter?" the doctor asked Mary Delany, who was sitting in the emergency room waiting area. She nodded. A lump in her throat prevented her from responding. "He's coming around," the doctor informed her. She let out a big sigh of relief. Tears were running down her face.

"Did you need to talk to him first?" the doctor asked Art Keller, who had been sitting with Mary and Chloe Boyer in the waiting room on the 4th floor of St. Peter's Hospital.

"I can wait a bit longer," Keller answered. "Let his daughter see him first."

"Thank you," Mary said, getting to her feet while wiping her eyes with a tissue.

"This way," the doctor said, heading back through the swinging doors.

Mary had been half-expecting a call to come some day to say her father had suffered a stroke or a heart attack. He was trying to keep his cholesterol and blood pressure down, but he needed to lose at least twenty pounds, and walking the dog twice a day was hardly exercise. She had been nervous when he told her about meeting Dr. Johns in the park, but he made it seem like nothing bad could happen. She feared the worst when the call came telling her that her father was being taken to St. Peter's.

When she entered the room, she saw her father in bed with an oxygen mask over his mouth and nose, with tubes taped to his left arm. She felt light-headed herself.

"You okay, Mrs. Delany?" the doctor asked.

She nodded. She noticed the monitoring devices that were stacked along the wall. The lines were moving.

"Let me explain what's going on with your father," the doctor said after moving to the opposite side of the bed.

Mary turned to face the doctor, whose name according to the badge on his white jacket was Dr. Vikram. "Your father consumed something—possibly epinephrine—which spiked his heart rate, causing him to become disoriented. Because of the medications he is taking, he might have suffered serious harm, possibly even a cerebral hemorrhage."

He consulted his clipboard. "The ambulance crew reported that your father was about a half a mile from the parking lot at the Thatcher Park. By the time they reached him, he was unconscious, but they were able to revive him and his heart rate is now almost back to normal."

Mary knew most of the latter, having been briefed by Chloe Boyer when she arrived at the hospital. Chloe explained that her role was to stay within range of the microphone Jake had hidden in his jacket, but to stay out of sight. When she lost voice contact, she realized that Dr. Johns must have taken them up the trail so far that her receiver was out of range. Trying not to panic, Chloe drove her car up to the highest elevation parking lot in hopes of picking up their conversation. Fortunately, she was able to re-establish communications in time to learn that Mary's father was in trouble. Then, however, she had to drive back down to the park entrance and alert the park ranger because she wasn't able to establish any cell-phone service.

"All indications are that he's going to be fine," the doctor said, "but we won't know if there was any damage until we're able to do some additional tests. We'll keep him for at least twenty-four hours, but I thought it would be good for him to know that you're here."

Mary nodded and moved closer to her father. He had never seemed so small to her as he was at that moment lying there. His eyes were closed.

"Is he conscious?" she asked.

"Yes. I believe so," the doctor replied. He lifted the oxygen mask so Jake could talk.

"Hi, Mary?" Jake said, opening his eyes.

"You've given us all quite a scare, Dad."

Jake nodded his head slightly. "Me too."

"The doctor says you're going to make it."

Jake's eyelids fluttered. "Nice to know," he said.

"Lieutenant Keller is outside and would like to see you," the doctor said. "I'm inclined to tell him to come back tomorrow, but it's up to you."

"No. It's okay. Send him in."

The doctor left to get Keller. Mary put her hand on top of her father's hand, but had to pull it away to reach into her pocketbook for a tissue to dab her eyes.

"I'm sorry, Dad," she said, tears coming down her checks. "I just hate to see you this way."

"Don't worry. I'll be okay," Jake replied in a voice barely above a whisper.

"Should I leave?" Mary asked when Art Keller entered the room.

"That's not necessary," Keller said. "How are you feeling, Jake?"

"Been better."

"I'm sure. I came by to tell you we arrested Bernard Johns. He's downtown blabbing like a parrot. Admitted to killing both Feldman and Lunsford. Said he might as well give us the details because you'd find them out eventually."

Jake tried to smile. "Amazing. What about Angela Boyer?"

"Claims he had nothing to do with her death, but we'll keep pushing him."

Jake nodded.

"I'll need to hear what you've got—when you get out of here, of course," Keller said.

"Sure thing," Jake said.

"Anyway, all the guys downtown want you to know that they're pulling for you."

"Thanks," Jake said.

Keller nodded to Mary and the doctor and left the room. Mary had stopped crying. She felt proud—as proud of her father as she'd ever felt.

Jake appeared to be sleeping when Mary arrived the next morning. The TV was on, but without any sound. She hesitated, but he opened his eyes.

"Hi there," he said.

"Hi. How are you doing?"

"They wore me out with a bunch of tests this morning. There's nothing good on TV, so I thought I'd take a nap."

"Did the doctor say when you can come home?" Mary asked.

"I don't know. I haven't seen anyone but the nurses since they brought me back here."

"I brought you something," Mary said.

"What's that?"

Mary pulled a copy of that day's Albany Times out of her pocketbook. She opened it up to show her father. The heading for the lead story read, Dentist Confesses To Murder.

"Amazing," Jake said, shaking his head in disbelief.

"I'll leave it with you," Mary said, "but let me read you one sentence. Let's see, where is it . . . Oh, here we go. Ready?"

Jake nodded.

"'Johns' arrest, according to Chief of Police Jennings,'" Mary read, "'came about as a result of the detective work of former Albany police officer Robert Barnes. Jennings stated that he would send a request to the Common Council for a commendation for Barnes, without whose efforts Bernard Johns might never have been apprehended.'"

"Wish they'd listened to me a few years ago," Jake said.

Mary nodded. "But you always say—"

"I know. I always say they've got too many cases to deal with. But they ought to listen to the guys who are on the job."

"So, now what, Dad?" Mary asked. "You had enough?"

"We'll see," Jake said. "Maybe I'll go visit Ed Marshall in Florida after New Year's. But as long as I'm living here in Albany, I might as well make myself useful."

Mary smiled. She knew better than to argue. It wouldn't do any good anyway.

Later that day Jake opened his eyes and was surprised to see Chloe Boyer standing by the window.

"How's the weather?" he asked.

She turned around. "It's raining."

"Guess I owe you my thanks," Jake said. "You saved my life."

"I told you that you wouldn't regret hiring me."

Jake smiled. "Well, the price was right."

She laughed, but then got a sad look on her face. "Johns says he didn't have anything to do with Angela's getting meningitis."

"I read that in the paper," Jake said. "I don't know whether or not to believe him."

"He confessed to killing those other women," Chloe said. "Doesn't that mean he killed Angela, too?"

Jake nodded. "I don't know what to tell you, Chloe."

"Maybe he didn't do it," she said, "but if you hadn't tried to find out, he would have gotten away with the other two."

"I guess that's the silver lining," Jake admitted. "Has your dad said anything about it?"

"He did. He called me when the story broke. He wants to meet with you when you're out so he can apologize."

"He doesn't have anything to apologize for," Jake said. "I'm not sure I would have responded any differently if I'd been in his shoes. I didn't have a lot to go on other than my belief that Johns was a killer."

"He should have hired you anyway. You weren't asking for a lot of money."

"But then I wouldn't have had you for a partner," Jake said.

Chloe laughed. "Pain-in-the-butt assistant is what I was most of the time."

"But you came through in the end, Chloe, and that's what counts. Say, don't you have some shopping to do?"

"Come to think of it Mary told me about this new line in her store. I think I'll go take a look."

"Thanks for coming in," Jake said.

"You'd better come to my wedding," Chloe said. "You and Mary, both. Next June."

"I'll be there," Jake replied. "I love a good wedding."

Peter G. Pollak

27

Thursday, September 23: 9:15 a.m.

Jake heard the phone ringing as he let Benji into the house after their morning walk. He taken the long route that morning and felt stronger than he'd felt since before the incident in Thatcher Park.

"Jake Barnes," he answered, not sure if he'd reached the phone before the caller hung up.

"Jake. It's Curt. Curt Ellis."

"Hey, Curt, how are things?"

"Good, and you?"

"Never better. What's up?"

"I need some help if you think you're up to it."

"Sure. What can I do for you?"

"Help me on a surveillance. I'm running a twenty-four hour watch on one of Albany's leading politicians and need some one who knows his stuff so the guy doesn't catch on that he's being watched."

"I think I could do that, but is it just the two of us?"

Curt laughed. "No, I've got two other guys who are going to help out."

"Perfect. When do we start?"

"Right away. Can you come down to my office later this morning? I'll introduce you to the other guys and we'll work out our schedule."

"Give me an hour. I've got to shower and get dressed."

"Excellent. See you then."

Jake hung up the phone. Benji was waiting by his water bowl. Jake filled it up and patted the dog on the head. "Got to leave you alone for a while, old girl," he said to the dog. "Seems like I'm needed around Albany after all."

ABOUT THE AUTHOR

In the Game is Peter G. Pollak's fourth self-published novel. It takes place in time before *Making the Grade* (2012), which is also set in Albany, New York where Pollak lived for forty years.

His first novel, *The Expendable Man* (2011) is a political thriller that takes place in Albany and elsewhere. Novel number three, *Last Stop on Desolation Ridge* (2013) is a suspense that takes place in the Adirondacks in Upstate New York.

All four novels are available in e-book and paperback editions.

To stay current on Pollak's writing projects, sign up for his e-newsletter on his website at www.petergpollak.com and for his Write or Wrong blog where he posts reviews of books he's reading as well as news about writing.

Before getting serious about writing fiction, Pollak was a journalist, educator, lobbyist and entrepreneur.

Pollak was born in Northville, New York, but grew up in Gloversville, New York.

He earned a B.A. from Oberlin College, a M.A. in American History from the University at Albany, and a Ph.D. in History and Education from the University of Albany.

He is married and has two children and four grandchildren.

Made in the USA
Columbia, SC
22 June 2017